Toys and Tales by Edie Kraska
from Grandmother's Attic

Houghton Mifflin Company
Boston, Massachusetts
1979

published for the
Boston Children's Museum

For Lanie, Edie and Joy

Illustrated and designed by Edie Kraska and Peter Kemble. Color photography by Philip Jon Bailey.

Typeset in Memphis and Century Schoolbook Bold Linofilm.

Printed in the United States of America.
10 9 8 7 6 5 4 3 2 1

Library of Congress Cataloging in Publication Data

Kraska, Edie.
 Toys and tales from grandmother's attic.

 Bibliography: p.
 SUMMARY: Recounts the history of 15 toys and folk-art crafts from the collection of the Boston Children's Museum and provides instructions for making them.
 1. Handicraft—Juvenile literature. 2. Toy making—Juvenile literature. 3. Toys—History—Juvenile literature. 4. Folk art—History—Juvenile literature. [1. Handicraft. 2. Toy making. 3. Toys—History. 4. Folk art—History] I. Boston. Children's Museum. II. Title.
 TT160.K73   745.59′2   79-9052
 ISBN 0-395-27807-4   ISBN 0-395-28582-8 pbk.

Many people helped me with this book. I would first like to thank the Children's Museum and Michael Spock, the Director, for making the Collection available to me. Jim Zien helped enormously by encouraging me to develop my initial ideas. His backing was instrumental in getting the project going, and his suggestions were extremely useful. Joan Lester was especially helpful in explaining the Native American Collection and pointing out sources for more information. Sonnet Takahisa shared her knowledge of the Japanese toys I selected and told me about Girl's Day Festival. Ruth Green suggested source material on the Pantins and, with Joan Lester, read the entire manuscript, making suggestions and comments. Sylvia Sawin, Karen Anne Zien, and Judy Battat made many good suggestions. I'd also like to thank Julia Sheehan and Phyllis Van Wart for their help with the Collection, and Ruth Anne Bacon, Virginia Boyd, Ellie Lander, and Marlene Levine for additional illustrations and examples of some of the toys and crafts.

Pawel Depta, of the Cambridge Public Library, told me his recollections of Wycinan and recommended sources for research. The Polish Cultural Club let me use its library. The Polish Embassy and the Eastman Kodak Company kindly sent me much useful graph material. Philip Bailey's help and cooperatio in photographing the objects were especiall important.

I would also like to thank two of my specia friends. Peter Kemble encouraged me throug out the writing of this book and gave me his unfailing support, guidance, worthwhile advice, and criticism. I would like to thank him especially for his efforts. Michael Morar who read and reread the manuscript in prog ress, gave me encouragement at times when I needed it most.

Toys and Tales from Grandmother's Attic

Introduction

▲ Kids dressing up in old clothes in Grandmother's Attic.

Grandmother's Attic is an exhibit in the Boston Children's Museum. I remember the first time I came upon this appealing replica of a Victorian attic with its antique toys and treasures. As the Museum's graphic designer, I was accustomed to finding unexpected visual surprises—like pieces of old exhibits stored in out-of-the-way places—and so I was charmed by the ingenious and colorful objects on display, many of which came from the Museum's Collection. But I was really unprepared to discover the multitude of wonderful toys stored away in the Collection itself. Here I found folk-toys and crafts, many over one hundred years old, from every corner of the globe. There were over fifty thousand objects, and those kept in countless trays and boxes were as interesting as those I had seen in Grandmother's Attic. They brought back memories of my childhood and rekindled my interest in toys.

My interest increased as I worked on new Museum exhibits which showed toys from the Collection. "If I Were a Kid Back Then," an exhibit about the history of children in the United States, displayed many early American toys. Other exhibits were of toys and crafts of children from different countries and cultures. While working on these exhibits I had a chance to look at many of these toys more closely, and began to wonder about how they were once used and about the craftspeople who made them. I decided on a project: I would select some of the most appealing toys and crafts, write a book which told something of their history and origins, and photograph them so that a working reproduction could be made of each one. I envisioned a book that children and their parents could enjoy together, each discovering something about toys and the fun of making them, teaching and learning from each other in the process.

Some of the objects I chose were very old; others were more recent. Some came from this country, while others were from unfamiliar lands far away. Many of the toys I selected—particularly the puppets—were used to tell or perform folk tales or plays. I included examples of these tales and plays wherever possible, to show the toys in the context of their cultures.

Children often wonder who made their toys, where their games came from, who thought up the pointed cap on their favorite puppet. Anthropologists, psychologists, collectors and historians of toys ask the same questions because the origin and history of toys tell a great deal about people and the way they live. Most of the antique toys and crafts in this book occupied different niches and served different purposes in their times than toys do now. Their differences and similarities make an interesting story.

Many early toys were designed not only for children but for adults as well. Itinerant showmen employed Shadow Puppets to illu-

▲ *A few of the many toys, dolls, and miscellaneous curious objects in Grandmother's Attic.*

trate allegorical tales and religious stories for audiences young and old who could seldom read and write. These enchanting puppets were really a form of mass communication and entertainment long before radio, television, magazines, or movies. But they were more than entertainment: They helped transmit and preserve the legends and literature of their people. In the twentieth century, with the inexpensive availability of mass media, the role that folk-toys filled has steadily diminished. These objects were once communicators of tradition, but in the twinkle of a technological age they have become historical curiosities.

Other toys passed along traditions in other ways. The Japanese Festival Dolls were used to instruct children in the customs and manners of the Imperial Court. Some modern dolls serve the same function: They help children understand and practice adult roles. But few modern toys teach children anything of tradition, perhaps because traditions are less important in a rapidly changing age than they once were.

Some toys became popular fads to a degree which seems improbable today. The Pantins were elegant French puppets acquired by the nobility, and they came to be only too expressive of aristocratic life. They remain fascinating after two hundred years because they symbolize the tastes and fashions of eighteenth-century France. The Brownies achieved equal popularity, though they were never the same symbols of status. They anticipated the now common association between popular culture and advertising. These elves originated in Scottish folklore and wound up not only winning the hearts and minds of children but promoting cameras and oranges!

Of course many toys have always been primarily for fun and entertainment. Punch and Judy were puppets which delighted crowds at the ubiquitous country fairs and at street theater performances in cities across Europe. They put on a slapstick show, without the subtlety or grace of the shadow puppets, but they were a great catharsis and allowed people to see their wishes and desires acted out on stage in ways that would have been socially unacceptable in real life. Like the Shadow Puppets, Punch and Judy have been eclipsed by movies and TV.

The moving picture toys have no exact equivalent today. They are an outgrowth of the nineteenth-century interest in "natural philosophy," as physics was then called. The toys were really scientific experiments brought into the parlor to delight both children and grownups. The devices were educational as well as entertaining. But today science has advanced so far beyond the ken or forecast of the nineteenth century that it is hardly possible to have toys demonstrate new scientific principles. Instead we play games with toys which are miniature electronic computers, but we have scant understanding of how they work. Perhaps for that reason these toys have lost some of the charm antique toys retain.

Many other toys used ingenious mechanical principles. The Lazy Tongs toy, with its scissors handle, has an almost Rube Goldberg quality, like many other nineteenth-century toys which use levers, wheels, screws, and springs to run, jump, skip, or place money in a bank. Toy designers were not averse to gimmicks, especially when they produced surprises. One designer even produced a toy box containing a wooden snake; when a child slid open the top, the snake, which had a nail for a tongue, darted out to hit his finger!

Traditional crafts, like early toys, appeal to us for many reasons. We usually understand the manufacturing processes and can appreciate the skills involved in making these objects. The hand of the designer is everywhere evident in the product, and the eye is not misled by superfluous effects. Materials are used in ways which are consistent with their intrinsic properties. And most traditional crafts fulfill a real need, with their form clearly related to their function, whether that function is ornamental or utilitarian.

Paper cut-outs made in many parts of the world are good examples of crafts that are both functional and decorative. The Polish cut-outs and the Mexican stencils were—and still are—inexpensive, colorful, and joyful forms of decoration using familiar themes from everyday life. When pasted on windows they filter sunlight and provide privacy. These cut-outs and stencils are particularly attractive because they are recognizable and appealing designs elegantly executed with simple means and materials.

The Passamaquoddy Indians used materials in ingenious ways to make birchbark baskets. The baskets were folded from a single piece of bark held together with spruce roots. Some baskets and boxes were decorated with figures from Passamaquoddy legends. Many other legends and folk-tales have been the inspiration for other craft objects. Characters from the Japanese tale of the Tongue-cut Sparrow were carved as small wooden figures, hand painted on glass slides, or delicately illustrated on story cards.

Some folk-art toys and crafts were fore-runners of mass-produced objects. Noah's Ark was made by groups of craftsmen, each of whom had a specific task in its manufacture. However, these arks never lost their handmade character. The ark was a "Sunday Toy," revealing the rather severe attitude which many people in the nineteenth century had toward religion and play. Children were only allowed to play with the ark on Sunday, and then only to learn or tell the story of the Flood.

The toys and crafts in this book are all products of their times and the countries that produced them. Because these times and places differed from ours, these objects express that difference. But there are also similarities, since children and adults everywhere have common desires and fantasies. People have always had heroes to applaud and villains to denounce. Our heroes might seem strange to our ancestors, but not our hero worship. We are fascinated by TV and movie stars and by astronauts and athletes. Our toys and games often center around these figures.

We also like toys that make us laugh and cry and toys we can take care of. We like toys that move, toys that test our skill, and toys that stretch our imagination.

What contemporary toys will collectors exhibit in a hundred years? Perhaps some that seem banal today will be treasured tomorrow. The Children's Museum has recently added a scaled-down version of Evel Knievel on his motorcycle to its Collection of American toys. Come for a visit next century and see if it's on display!

The Children's Museum is in its new home on Fort Point Channel in Boston. When you come, you can't miss the 40-foot-high milk bottle outside the building! The Museum is in a renovated warehouse and has many new exhibits. Grandmother's Attic has been expanded as part of "City Slice," which show a section through an entire house and the cellar and street below. Other exhibits will show many more toys, crafts, and other objects from the Collection.

I hope the objects in this book inspire you to create some of your own toys and crafts, tales and plays. Perhaps you will fold your own origami dolls, design wonderful new shadow puppets, or cut out your own colorful stencils to decorate your walls and windows. Perhaps you will create new and fantastic animals for Noah's Ark, or draw Zoetrope strips or flip cards and make your own moving pictures. Maybe you will design a toy future generations will treasure and tell stories about.

I hope you will enjoy making and reading about these toys and crafts as much as I have. And most of all, I hope you have as much fun with them as their original owners surely had so long ago!

▼ *A beautiful nineteenth century doll from the Museum's Collection.*

Moving Picture Toys

▲ *A drawing of a spinning Thaumatrope showing the front and back images superimposed.*

The eye momentarily retains the image of an object after the object is removed from sight. This principle, the persistence of vision, had been known since the days of Ptolemy in the second century A. D., but for nearly seventeen hundred years remained a phenomenon with no practical applications.

In 1824 the English physician and scientist P. M. Roget, who later was to write the well-known Thesaurus bearing his name, began experimenting with persistence of vision. His work, and that of many other inventors and tinkerers, led to an outpouring of optical toys and mechanical devices that were ingenious and frequently charming and comical. Among these were the Thaumatrope, the Phenakistoscope, and the Zoetrope. These toys, often with Greek or Latin names that seem slightly bizarre or quaint today, captivated adults and children alike. The application of the principle of persistence of vision ultimately led to the development of motion pictures.

Thaumatrope

Probably the earliest toy to use the persistence of vision principle was the Thaumatrope (thaw'-ma-trope). Beginning about 1826, five different people claimed that they invented this gadget. It was the ultimate in simplicity, consisting merely of a disk with strings tied at opposite points on the circumference. When the strings were twisted and pulled the disk spun around. An image was drawn or printed on each side, and these images would appear superimposed as the disk rotated. Thus a bird might be printed on one side and a cage on the other; when the disk turned the bird would appear to be inside the cage.

How to make a Thaumatrope

1. Cut a 2″ cardboard disk and punch two holes at opposite points on the circumference.

2. Draw an image on each side of the disk; when superimposed they should make a complete picture. For example, on one side a bird, on the reverse a cage; or, on one side a horse, on the reverse a rider. The image on the front should be right side up; on the back, upside down.

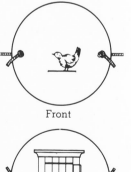

Front

3. Tie a string in each hole and twist. Pull the twisted string so the disk spins; the images on each side will appear superimposed.

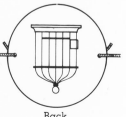

Back

Phenakistoscope

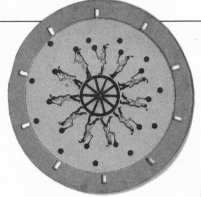

The Phenakistoscope (fen-a-kist'-o-scope) was probably the earliest toy to produce the effect of moving pictures. This nineteenth-century word is a combination of *phenakisto*, from the Greek meaning "to trick," and *scope*, from the Latin "to examine." The toy was invented in 1832 by Joseph Plateau, a Belgian who became partially blind testing his persistence of vision. He stared at the sun for twenty seconds, and the image of the sun seemed to remain in his eyes because the sun's ultraviolet rays burned holes in his retina! Persistence of vision had nothing to do with it.

The Phenakistoscope was a cardboard disk with a series of radial drawings, for example, of a girl jumping rope. Each drawing showed the girl at a different moment. Slits were cut into the disk next to each drawing. The disk was held in front of a mirror and rotated as the operator looked through the moving slits; the reflection appeared to show a continuous moving picture of the girl jumping.

The Phenakistoscope was a much more sophisticated idea than the Thaumatrope and foreshadowed a wide range of toys, all using a series of drawings but incorporating different methods to make them appear to move.

▲ *The Phenakistoscope holder and viewing disk came with several interchangeable disks printed with different images. Here a fiddler moves his bow as a dancer jumps up and down. The disks on the left show ladies dancing, a man batting a ball, a blacksmith working with a trip hammer, and two men leapfrogging.*

How to make a Phenakistoscope (use worksheets on pages 41–42)

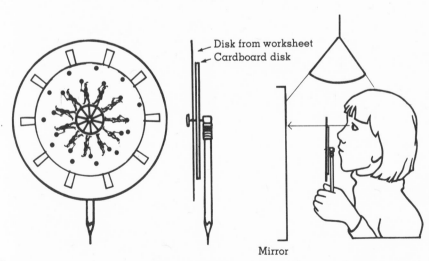

Disk from worksheet
Cardboard disk

Mirror

1. Cut out Phenakistoscope and punch a hole through the center. Cut out viewing slits.

2. Cut a circle 6" in diameter out of heavy cardboard and punch a hole through the center.

3. Place the Phenakistoscope on top of the cardboard circle and push a thumbtack through both holes into the side of an eraser on the top of a pencil. (You may put soap on the eraser before pushing in the tack to lessen friction.)

4. Hold the Phenakistoscope with the image side facing a mirror.

Place a light to illuminate the drawings. Look through the viewing slits and spin the disk; the reflected pictures in the mirror will appear to move.

To make your own drawings move:

1. Cut a circle 6" in diameter out of heavy paper and place on top of the Phenakistoscope with viewing slits.

2. Draw straight lines to connect opposite viewing slits. You will have made a series of pie-shaped frames, as shown.

3. Draw a series of images in the frames, each slightly different from the preceding image. Spin the disk and your drawings will appear to move!

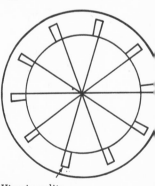

Viewing slits

Zoetrope

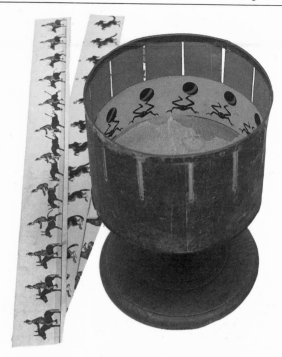

The Zoetrope (zó-e-trope) is another optical toy that produced the effect of motion pictures. Surprisingly, this curious-looking device was invented twice: first in 1834 by William Horner and again in 1860 by Pierre Deşvigns. The French called it Zoetrope, meaning "wheel of life."

The Zoetrope and the Phenakistoscope are similar in their methods of operation. Both combine a spinning surface with slits for viewing a series of drawings. Instead of the paper disk used in the Phenakistoscope, the Zoetrope used a metal cylinder. Equidistant slits were cut around the circumference. Each image showing each moment of action was drawn on a long horizontal strip that fit inside the cylinder. By rotating the cylinder and looking through the moving slits the viewer saw the illusion of a continuously moving picture.

In 1878 Eadweard Muybridge used the Zoetrope in an ingenious experiment to help win a bet. Governor Leland Stanford of California, the founder of Stanford University and a great admirer of horses, wagered $25,000 that a galloping horse has all four feet off the ground at the same instant. He asked Muybridge—who had been experimenting with photo-

▲ *This Zoetrope drum and stand were sold along with ten cartoon strips with drawings on both sides. The cartoons had humorous titles: "Raining Pitchforks," "Kick Her Up," and "Keep the Ball Rolling."*

How to make a Zoetrope (use worksheets on pages 43–44)

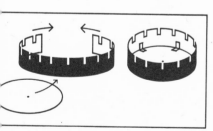

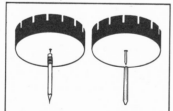

1. Cut a circle 6³/₈″ in diameter out of heavy cardboard and punch a small hole through the center.

2. Cut out the black strip and tape the ends together. Tape tab A over A¹. The other two ends B and B¹ butt together. The black side should face out. Be sure to cut the viewing slits before taping.

3. Place the strip on the cardboard circle and carefully tape the pieces together.

4. Put an eightpenny or tenpenny nail through the center of the cardboard circle into the end of a ball-point pen barrel, or push a thumbtack through the circle into an eraser on the top of a pencil. (Put soap on the top of the eraser before pushing in tack to lessen friction.)

5. Place the Zoetrope strip inside drum. The pictures should face the center of the drum. Hold the Zoetrope under a light and look through the viewing slits at the frame directly opposite you. Spin the drum and the pictures will appear to move.

To make your own cartoon strips:

1. Cut out a strip of paper 1¹¹/₁₆″ x 20¹/₈″ long.

2. Divide the strip into 12 equal frames by drawing lines every 1¹¹/₁₆″.

3. Draw a series of sequential images in the frames. See how many different ideas for moving pictures you can draw!

▲ *A girl peeks through the slits of a Zoetrope drum as she spins it to animate her stick figure drawings.*

Kineograph

graphy to study motion in animals and people — to help prove him right. Muybridge lined up a series of cameras along a race track. As a horse galloped past, each camera photographed the horse at a different moment in its stride. The sequence of photos clearly showed that at one point the horse did have all its feet off the ground. By placing these pictures in a Zoetrope and spinning the drum, Muybridge became the first person to use photographs to make a real motion picture, and also helped Stanford win his bet.

Milton Bradley, the American toy manufacturer, thought the Zoetrope would sell well in this country. In 1867 he produced his own version of the toy. Several years later Bradley thought of a way to reduce production costs and sell the toy for less; he made Zoetrope cylinders from the round hat boxes used by haberdashery firms.

The Zoetrope became the most popular early optical toy and paper strips were made to display an enormous variety of whimsical, comical, and sometimes grotesque moving images. There was a simple and light-hearted appeal to the Zoetrope strip cartoon characters' performance of slapstick and comic routines. These comic figures were the great-grandparents of the characters in contemporary movie cartoons.

The Kineograph (kin'-e-o-graph) or flipbook is another simple toy used to simulate moving pictures. It was patented in 1868, but probably had existed for many years before. Some school children were probably clever enough to think of this idea long before it was first patented.

The Kineograph is simply a pad of pictures, each page showing one image in a sequential series. The image is retained by the eye for a brief instant between the flip of one page to another.

The Mutascope is a mechanical device to hold the cards that are viewed by turning a crank that flips the pictures. With the manufacture of Mutascope peepshows, movie parlors spread across the United States and Europe at the turn of the century. The peepshows offered a variety of spectacular moving pictures: cops and robbers, comedy acts, and cartoons. Moving pictures came out of the Victorian sitting room, where only a fortunate few played with this optical toy, and into the public penny arcade lined with rows of Mutascopes, where many more people could view them.

How to make a Kineograph (use worksheets on pages 45-46)

▲ *A girl looks at the flip cards in a Mutascope machine at the Children's Museum.*

1. Cut out picture cards and place one on top of the other to make a pad. Start with one and arrange in numerical order to 15.

2. Put a rubber band around the stack of cards to hold them together. The rubber band fits into the notches.

3. Flip the pages and the pictures will appear to move.

To make your own flip cards:

1. Draw a series of sequential images on equal-sized cards. Some examples might be:
• A figure running or jumping.
• A flower growing.
• A spaceship crossing the sky.
• Smoke coming out of a chimne

Puppets and Dolls

▲ *This Shadow Puppet horse could gallop across the shadow screen, perhaps carrying its rider in search of romance or adventure.*

For thousands of years man has made puppets and dolls in his own image and in the image of his gods and godesses, heroes and ancestors. Dolls and puppets were the recipients of affection and hostility, and they kept the company of young and old, both in life and often buried with their owners — after death. Then dolls became actors. Puppets were used to play legendary characters on the stage and were an effective and entertaining way of giving life to myths and legends for audiences in preliterate societies. Some dolls were used to portray powerful figures in court or government, thus becoming a way to teach children history and etiquette. Dolls were often as dear to adults as to children; some became adult fads that enjoyed unprecedented popularity.

This is the story of several wonderful puppets and dolls from around the world. After you've read about them, you may want to design your own dolls, or add new characters to the shadow puppets illustrated here and on the worksheets at the back of the book.

Shadow Puppets

Shadow puppets are an artistic and theatrical invention over twenty centuries old. Originally shadow puppets were not really toys but were an elegant means by which skillful puppet masters presented epic folk and religious tales. The rooster-like bird on the next page is a Chinese shadow puppet over one hundred years old. When lit from behind, its translucent body allows projected light to pass through, creating a wonderful effect of colored images flickering across a screen which is also translucent. The audience sits in front of the screen and never sees the actual puppets, but views the entire performance as moving colored shadows. The colored shadows projected from these puppets, and the puppets themselves, are as fascinating today as they undoubtedly were to peasants and aristocrats two thousand years ago.

Some people believe the idea for shadow puppets first came from seeing shadows cast on the paper screens that divide the rooms in Asian houses. Others think the idea came from seeing shadows cast on the sides of tents of nomadic tribes. Shadow theater may have begun in China or in India, but the puppets are so different in appearance that shadow theater probably developed independently in both countries. The history of Chinese shadow theater may have begun in the Han Dynasty (206 B.C.–A.D. 221), but the true origins can now be traced only through legends. The tale of the Emperor Wu-ti is typical. He became

inconsolable at the death of his consort, and
Taoist priest offered to make her image
reappear. The priest accomplished this by
projecting a female silhouette on a screen,
much to the Emperor's satisfaction. This
legend involving the Taoist priest as shadow
master illustrates the early associations
Chinese shadow theater had with religion;
the elusive and dreamlike quality of the
puppets' shadows reinforced the spiritual and
supernatural quality of the performances.
The Chinese called the screen on which the
shadows were cast the "screen of death."

The earliest written records of the Chinese
shadow plays appear in the *T'an-su* — the
massive five-thousand-volume Chinese
encyclopedia written in the eleventh century
— which documents shadow theater in the
Sung Dynasty (A.D. 960–1280), a period noted
for its literature and art.

Shadow plays were a source of entertainment and instruction for audiences that were
largely illiterate, with little education or
exposure to the arts. The plays came to portray
not only religious themes but also stories of
romance, heroism, morality and history. The
most frequently performed plays centered
around the Eight Immortals, gods who fought
off the forces of evil. Evil was personified by
demons who could transform themselves into
monsters and dragons waging war against
the Immortals, or disguise themselves as
beautiful women or handsome youths in an
attempt to trick the Immortals.

Shadows masters went from village to
village, performing plays from their reper-
toire. They carried puppets carefully packed
in a chest, along with a portable screen. The
three by five foot screen was originally made

◄ *This rooster is a Peking-style shadow puppet cut from
animal skin and painted with layers of color. When lit
from behind it casts its colored shadows onto a screen.*

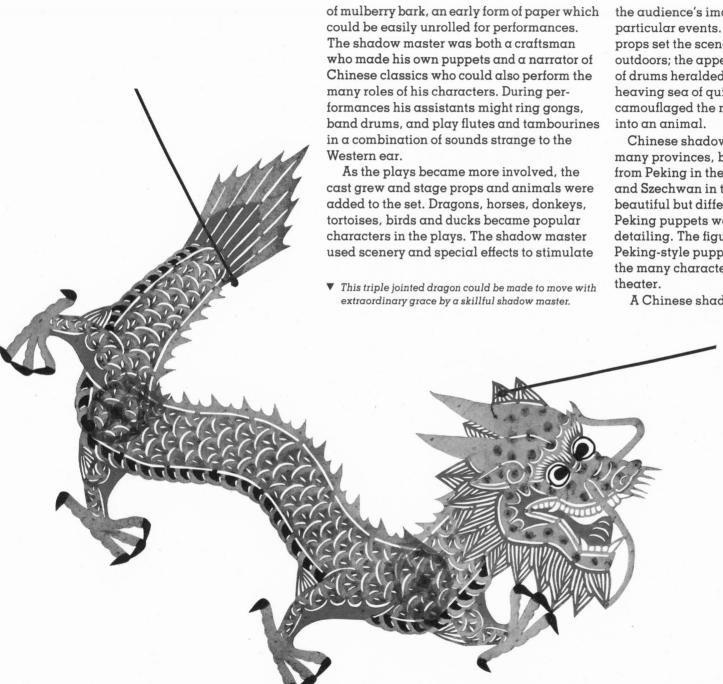

of mulberry bark, an early form of paper which could be easily unrolled for performances. The shadow master was both a craftsman who made his own puppets and a narrator of Chinese classics who could also perform the many roles of his characters. During performances his assistants might ring gongs, band drums, and play flutes and tambourines in a combination of sounds strange to the Western ear.

As the plays became more involved, the cast grew and stage props and animals were added to the set. Dragons, horses, donkeys, tortoises, birds and ducks became popular characters in the plays. The shadow master used scenery and special effects to stimulate

▼ *This triple jointed dragon could be made to move with extraordinary grace by a skillful shadow master.*

the audience's imagination and to symbolize particular events. A few carefully selected props set the scene: a pagoda suggested the outdoors; the appearance of clouds and a roll of drums heralded a storm; a boat sailed on a heaving sea of quivering streamers. Smoke camouflaged the metamorphosis of a spirit into an animal.

Chinese shadow puppets were made in many provinces, but the most prominent came from Peking in the north, Canton in the south and Szechwan in the west. They were equally beautiful but differed in size and style. The Peking puppets were smaller and had finer detailing. The figures shown here are all Peking-style puppets; they are only a few of the many characters in the Chinese shadow theater.

A Chinese shadow master often owned

over one hundred figures and one thousand heads. Heads and bodies were interchangeable to provide an almost unlimited combination of personalities and characters. Each part of a puppet had symbolic importance: a black face indicated honesty and strength, a broad nose expressed wisdom and power, a fine nose with delicate features depicted nobility, and a cluster of arrows on the back of a figure meant status and importance. Servants, soldiers, princes, princesses, monks, monsters and demons were all part of the cast. A shadow master could manipulate figures to bow, kneel and sit down with extraordinary grace.

Making shadow puppets was a careful and exacting art. The shadow master used the skins of sheep, donkeys, water buffalo, and sometimes even certain kinds of fish. But donkey skin was preferred because it was thinner, more transparent and very durable. The master selected thicker skins for the body, thinner skins for the arms and legs. It was important to have the design of the puppet work with the grain of the hide to prevent warping. Very old shadow puppets

are flawlessly flat if the artist was careful. The shadow master meticulously cut each part of his puppet; a puppet often had ten or more pieces and a detachable head which fit into a collar on the puppet's neck. Small pieces of string were passed through tiny holes and knotted on both sides to connect the parts. The shadow master attached rods of bamboo, wood or ivory to wires which connected at the neck and hands to manipulate the puppet from below.

The shadow master worked his puppets from behind the screen while the audience sat in front. Originally kerosene lamps from behind the puppets cast their colored shadows on the screen. Much later, light bulbs replaced the lamps. The top of the screen slanted toward the audience and the shadow figures rested directly on the screen. At the bottom of the screen a wooden ledge supported the puppets' feet and legs and made manipulation of the figures easier.

Shadow masters taught their children and grandchildren the art of shadow play. Since this means of livelihood required long apprenticeship, the tradition of learning the

art extended over four or five generations of a family. Although shadow plays have lost much of their following, they are still performed. The Chang Teh-cheng Company presented a shadow puppet program to audiences throughout the United States in the 1960s. Chang is the fifth generation of a family of shadow masters, but his sons do not plan to follow in his footsteps.

In 1975 the Yueh Lung Shadow Theatre was organized in New York City and has given many performances in the United States and Europe.

Shadow puppet performances have a special magical quality like no other puppet show. The colored shadows are illusive and transitory; they flicker, become sharper, move with incredible alacrity, then suddenly fade and disappear. Their beauty, and the history and culture represented in their performance make them modern ambassadors from an ancient land.

▶ *In this camel, the overlapping animal skin is cut into pin-wheel shapes to allow more light to shine through.*

How to make Shadow Puppets (use worksheets on pages 47–54)

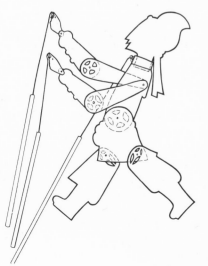

1. Cut out the shadow puppet parts and make tiny holes for the joints with a straight pin. If you wish you can cut out the white areas to allow more light to pass through your puppet.

2. Rub each piece with linseed oil to make the parts translucent. Allow the pieces to dry and then shellac them.

3. Connect all the parts by running string through the joint holes and tying knots on both sides.

4. Use wire and sticks or straws as rods, and attach to the puppet as shown. The main rod connects to the front collar, and a rod is connected to each hand. Hook the wire through the holes with a small loop.

5. To make a shadow screen, stretch a sheet across a doorway or use tracing paper glued to a picture frame.

6. The top of the screen should slant away from you; the shadow figures rest directly on the screen.

To make the collars for interchangeable puppet heads:

A	C	

1. Trace the collar pattern to make a collar for each shadow puppet figure.

2. Fold pattern where indicated and glue A to B.

3. Glue the neck of the puppet to C; the collar should be behind the neck of the puppet so it doesn't show.

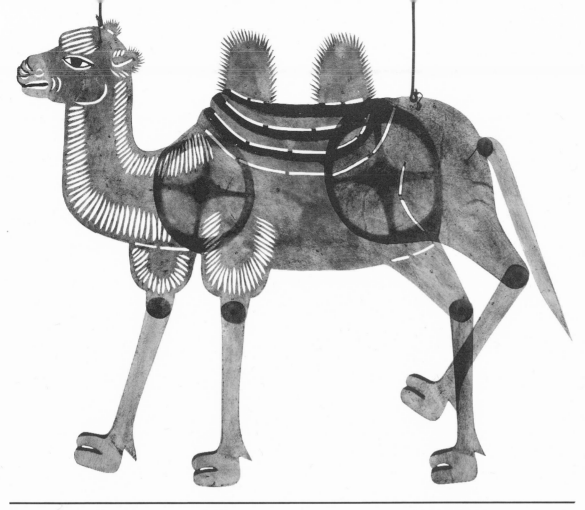

The Feast of Peaches

The Feast of Peaches is one of the classic Chinese shadow puppet plays. This play tells a tale of the Eight Immortals, who figure in endless Chinese legends and literature. The Eight Immortals are central figures in the accumulation of Taoist folklore and literature; they are evocations of the Tao belief that the attainment of spiritual enlightenment can be gained through harmony with nature. This play gives some feeling of the richness and grace of ancient Chinese culture even to those who have no knowledge of Taoism.

The Eight Immortals achieve their immortality through a study of nature's secrets. They reside in the heavenly domain of the Western Queen Mother and are ruled by her, but frequently pay visits to earthly mortals. Each Immortal is represented by an earthly character: a sage, a recluse, a handsome youth, and so on. Each carries a particular emblem: for example, a basket of flowers, a fly whisk, or a fan. They bestow happiness and long life on those they favor and are symbolic of all that is good.

The Western Queen controls the peach orchards filled with the Peaches of Immortality. The fruit ripens only once in three thousand years; when the peaches are ripe the Western Queen invites the Eight Immortals to her banquet to partake of the Peaches of Immortality as a reward for their enlightenment.

The play begins at the Western Queen's palace where the Feast of Peaches is taking place. There are amusements and gifts for the guests and a presentation of the Five Bats of Happiness who, when observed in flight, bring extraordinary joy to the beholder. At the end of the Feast, the Immortals decide that it is beneath their dignity to use an

To make horse's tail move:

1. Attach a stick or straw with string at the top and the bottom of the horse's saddle.

2. Tie one end of a piece of string around the stick about 1¾" from the bottom of the horse's saddle.

3. Attach the other end of the string to the horse's tail at hole marked D.

4. You can make the horse's tail move up and down by pulling the string with your finger while holding the stick.

ordinary boat to sail home across the sea. (Here the sea symbolizes the Sea of Life, with its many hazards.) They agree that each Immortal should travel on a cloud in the shape of his own emblem.

The next scene shows the Dragon Princess in her palace. She rules the streams, lakes and seas. The Dragon Princess has taken the form of a beautiful woman; she is angry because she has not been invited to the glorious Feast of Peaches. A crustacean messenger brings news to the Princess that the Eight Immortals, at that very moment, are

traversing her watery kingdom, and that there is one Immortal who carries a magic basket which can cause flowers to blossom at any season. To achieve her revenge, the Dragon Princess decides to capture this Immortal and gain possession of the magic flower basket.

The scene changes to show a sea of waves moving across the shadow screen. Below the watery surface the Dragon Princess's army of strange marine monsters lies in wait for the unsuspecting Immortals. Exaggerated forms of crayfish, carp, tortoises and octopi consti-

tute the undersea armada. The Immortals, crossing in single file, each on his own majestic cloud, skim the surface of the waves. All reach shore oblivious to the danger beneath them—that is, all but Han Hsiang-tzu who had lagged behind and was captured by the marine monsters.

The Immortals reassemble on the shore and discover that one among them is missing. Han Hsiang-tzu, the handsome youth, has met with foul play at the hands of the Dragon Princess! The Immortals consult the Book of Fate, which confirms their worst fears. But the Immortals are only slightly upset. "It is an occurrence of no importance," remarks Lu Tung-pin serenely. "We have only to request the Heavenly General, Er Lang, to lead the Celestial Armies to the rescue." A fierce battle erupts and the Heavenly General himself seeks out the Dragon Princess to teach her and her rebellious demons a lesson for their outrageous disrespect of the honorable Immortals. They engage in a terrible fight—figures fly across the screen! Finally the General entangles the Princess in a net. The beautiful woman is transformed into a resentful dragon and is led away to her judgement.

The seven Immortals draw their missing companion from the depths of the sea, still clutching his flower basket. They thank the Heavenly General and all depart in formal dignity, their ranks once again complete.

◆

Adapted by permission of the publishers from *Chinese Shadow Shows* by Genevieve Wimsatt, Cambridge, Mass.: Harvard University Press, Copyright © 1936 by the President and Fellows of Harvard College; renewed © 1964 by Genevieve Wimsatt.

◆

◀ *The delicate figure on the left is the Emperor; more commonly his clothes have a wave or water design to indicate he is a member of the Imperial Court. On the right is a peasant or fisherman.*

Pantins

Pantin puppets were a famous fad in eighteenth-century France. Each Pantin figure was printed in outline on sheets of paper and hand painted with water colors; its individual pieces were then cut apart, pasted on cardboard, and assembled. The Pantin was made to jump or dance by manipulating a single string attached to move its arms and legs in unison. Magistrates, harlequins, monks, fashionable society figures, and characters from the theater were portrayed as Pantins. The Pantin was originally a child's toy, but rapidly became a much sought after status symbol. The name may have come from the town of Pantin outside Paris.

The Pantin craze began with the aristocracy and spread throughout France, reaching a height of popularity in the decade between 1746 and 1756. The nobility had wealth and time to seek amusements in which to indulge themselves; they spent an inordinate amount of time and effort on clothes, fashions, manners, and on appearing at society salons and at the Palace of Versailles. Their passion for Pantins perhaps becomes understandable in this context, but a French writer, reflecting on the period before the French Revolution, wrote, "The nobility...played with Pantins and lapsed into childhood, while the people came of age!"

The Pantins were often beautifully drawn and colored by well-known French artists. They became so elegant that Pantin designs began to be imitated in women's fashions! François Boucher—court painter to Louis XV—produced Pantins which sold at high prices. Some members of the nobility spent large sums of money to acquire vast Pantin collections. One of Boucher's Pantins sold for 1500 livres, or over $300—an extraordinary amount of money at that time! Boucher's Pantins were drawn in the rococo style and were characterized by extraordinarily elaborate and delicate colors and lines. His Pantins reflected the grandiose and excessive court life of the reign of Louis XV.

The Pantin rage faded as quickly as it had blossomed, but the name remains in the French vocabulary. A person who vacillates, is indecisive, or is the puppet of another is called a pantin.

▲ Pierrette *is an itinerant minstrel and pantomime figure. This nineteenth-century design is more restrained than the earlier rococo Pantins.*

How to make a Pantin (use worksheet on page 56)

1. Cut out Pantin pieces from the worksheet and glue to cardboard to strengthen them. Punch out holes using a straight pin or hole punch.

2. Assemble the figure and attach parts using paper fasteners as shown, or a string knotted on both sides.

3. Tie a string to the top of each arm and tie another string to the top of each leg.

4. With a third piece of string connect the pieces as shown.

5. Tie a piece of string to the top of the head.

6. Hold the top string and pull the string below to make the Pantin move.

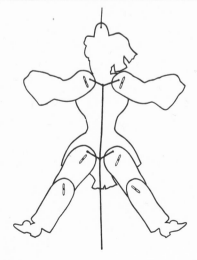

Punch and Judy

Pulcinella

Punch is the oldest and best-known puppet in Europe and America. This bizarre and brazen hunchback evolved over hundreds of years, appearing on stage in many forms and with many variations in different countries. He was played by both actors and puppets, originally in Greece and Rome and later in medieval minstrel shows and in country fairs and city street-theater.

Around 1600 an Italian actor who played this comic character named him Pulcinella, which may have derived from the Italian *pulcina* or "little chicken" because of the way in which he strutted across the stage. Pulcinella became known by similar names throughout Europe, as wandering puppeteers crisscrossed the continent. The British diarist Samuel Pepys (pronounced "Peeps") wrote that Pulcinella was introduced to England in 1662 by an Italian showman and described the details of a Pulcinella puppet show. In England the name Pulcinella became Punchinello, which was later shortened to Punch.

By the seventeenth century, Punchinello shows were playing at most of the great English country fairs: May Fair in the spring; Tottenham Court Fair; St. Bartholomew's Fair; and in the fall, Southwark Fair. Showmen set up their portable puppet theaters at these fairs and hung large posters to announce Punchinello's performances. An engraving by William Hogarth shows one of the posters advertising a morality play in which Punchinello dumps Vice from a wheelbarrow into the flaming mouth of a dragon.

Punchinello became Punch in the eighteenth century, and Judy and Baby were added to the cast. Punch and Judy shows became more and more popular and the puppet theater flourished as never before. The shows played to crowds all over London and in other European cities and began to be produced in the American colonies.

Punch combined characteristics from his varied origins; he sported a gigantic nose and protruding chin, and appeared even more singular because he often had a pronounced hunchback or sometimes vaguely camel-like crooked hump. In his early history Punch was merely an impudent or reckless comic figure, but in England he evolved into an obnoxious troublemaker creating mischief everywhere. As a popular puppet in street-theater, Punch became increasingly slapstick and vulgar to appeal to crowds and attract attention in the noisy London streets. Punch battled every character on the stage; the constable attempting to arrest him fell victim, as did the Devil himself. Perhaps Punch viewed the Devil as a rival!

In the seventeenth and eighteenth centuries Punch was usually a large and complex marionette manipulated by wires. Performances often required several showmen and considerable apparatus. But in the nineteenth century Punch more often took the form of a hand puppet, allowing one person to manipulate him rapidly as he fought the multitude of his adversaries. About this time the number of these adversaries increased as additional puppets joined the cast. Among the new arrivals were the Doctor, Jack Ketch the hangman, and Toby the dog. Sometimes a live dog substituted for the puppet! The showman attracted audiences by speaking loudly through a "swazzle" — a device which produced the shrill nasal voice that came to be identified with Punch. The showman might follow the outlines of a script, but he frequently varied the action according to the crowd's response. These technical and stylistic developments came at a fortuitous time because, by the beginning of the nineteenth century, Punch's popularity had finally begun to wane. The simpler and cheaper shows with greater

---

How to make a Punch and Judy Show (use worksheets on pages 60-61)

1. Cut out the Punch and Judy stage and the puppet figures from the worksheets.

2. Glue the figures to cardboard; extend the tabs so that they are longer than the ones on the worksheet.

3. Cut slits in the back of the stage where marked and insert the puppets from the front into the stage so that the tabs project below. You can manipulate the tabs to make the figures move.

4. You can add or remove characters to correspond to the action in the play. You might also want to improvise or make up your own lines.

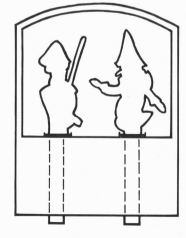

variety and action appealed to a wider audience and gave Punch and Judy renewed life.

Punch survived the competition of many other puppet characters because his appeal seems to have grown in proportion to his nastiness. Crowds responded to this sometimes comic, sometimes vulgar little figure who was always at odds with society. Punch probably acted out their fantasies, but the audience laughed knowing he was only a puppet, ready to pop up again to beat Judy with a stick or toss Baby out the window at the next performance.

Punch and Judy shows are still performed in England and occasionally in the United States. Though the shows are less popular than they once were, Punch can still be counted on to provide a comical and crowd-pleasing act.

In 1962, on the three hundredth anniversary of Punch's first performance in England, forty Punch showmen, their families, and their Toby dogs, converged on Covent Garden to commemorate the occasion. They unveiled a plaque proclaiming "Near this spot Punch's Puppet Show was first performed in England and was witnessed by Samuel Pepys, 1662." Plans are in the works for another commemorative celebration, perhaps before the four hundredth anniversary!

A Punch and Judy Play

The following Punch and Judy play has been adapted from an English children's book printed in 1859. The cover announces that it was played before the Queen at Windsor Castle, but it may have been shortened from the one presented to Queen Victoria because it contains only a few of the many characters common to most Punch and Judy plays. This version is unusual because Punch is caught in the end by the beadle, the minor parish official in English churches who keeps order and ushers during services. He is as much a symbol of order as Punch is of chaos.

Punch and Judy as played before the Queen

Enter PUNCH, singing:
> Rueete tuee, tu tu, rueete tuee ti.
> Oh I've just come before you
> To have a little game,
> My name, you know, is Punch,
> And it always was the same.

Judy, my dear, where's our pretty baby? I want to show him to my kind friends.

JUDY: Here he is, the little beauty, only look at his merry goggle eyes and his charming little hooked nose; I declare he's the very image of his handsome papa.

PUNCH: Ha, ha, ha! come here my sweet one, and let me teach you to dance and sing as well as I do myself. *(Sings.)*
> I'll dress him up like any king,
> On his finger I'll put a ring;
> Teach him to dance and then to sing
> Hoop de dooden doo.

Here's a beauty; only look at him—did you ever see such a picture before?

JUDY: Pray take care of him, Mr. Punch, and do not let him fall. *(Exit Judy.)*

PUNCH: Yes, my dear, I'll take great care of him. Ah! you little dear,
> Now you go up, up, up;
> Now you go downey, downey;
> Now you go backwards and forwards,
> And now you go—

Oh dear! oh dear! oh dear! I've let him fall. Oh! what will Judy say? *(Baby cries.)* Hush, my pretty, did it fall and hurt its little head? Poor fellow! Poor fellow! *(The baby cries still louder.)*

PUNCH: If you are not quiet, you little monkey, I'll beat you well. *(Punch lays the baby down and fetches a stick. He beats the child, who cries out much louder. At last he throws it out the window.)* There now, I've got rid of the noisy fellow at last. Oh, here comes Judy.

Enter JUDY: Come, Mr. Punch, let us have a dance. *(They both dance, and Punch sings.)*
> Ri ti tooty, ri tee too ti too.

JUDY: But what have you done with my darling child?

PUNCH: Why you see, Judy my dear, the baby was very naughty; so when I beat him, he cried, my dear; and then, you see, I knocked him on the head and threw him out the window; that's all, Judy dear.

JUDY: Oh, you wicked, wicked fellow, you've killed my pretty baby! Oh dear! oh dear! what shall I do?

PUNCH: There now; why anybody would think my Judy was cross. Don't be angry, dear. I'll soon tell you what to do; just be quiet, Judy my darling, or I must fetch my stick.

JUDY: Oh you brute.

PUNCH: Here's a pretty noise about the baby; why, anybody would think I had been ill-using him.

JUDY: You unfeeling brute, I'll go and fetch the beadle. He'll give you a lesson, Mr. Punch.

PUNCH: You may go; I don't care for the beadle. Who's afraid of him? *(Judy is going to run away, but Punch runs after her and beats her with his stick, until she lies quiet.)* There now, I've settled her. That's the way to stop her noise. Dear me, I hope I have not killed her. Judy, my dear, why don't you talk to me? *(Judy lies quiet, and Punch listens; at last he goes away.)*

◆

(Enter Dog Toby and Punch together.)
PUNCH: Toby, my fine little fellow, how are you?

TOBY: Bow, wow, wow.

PUNCH: Here's a pretty creature. How well he knows me. He's asking me how I do. I'll try to coax him. *(Punch stoops down to coax Toby, but Toby snaps at Punch's nose.)* Ah, you spiteful little dog, is that the way to treat your kind, loving master?

TOBY: Bow, wow, wow *(He bites his master's nose).*

PUNCH: Stop a bit; stop a bit, my little fellow; just sit up and tell all the good folks how old you are. *(Punch tries to make the dog sit up, but Toby bites his nose and makes him cry out with pain.)* Oh my nose; oh my nose. I'll punish you, Mr. Toby, for hurting me. *(Punch gets his stick and beats Toby, who runs away. Punch exits.)*

(Enter Beadle and Punch.)
BEADLE: Hello, Mr. Punch, I want you; you must go with me.

PUNCH: And pray who are you when you're at home?

BEADLE: Who am I? I'll soon tell you that: Why, I'm churchwarden, overseer, and beadle of the parish.

PUNCH: Well, Mr. Churchwarden, Overseer, and Beadle of the Parish, what do you want?

BEADLE: Why, I want you.

PUNCH: Want me? what do you want me for?

BEADLE: You have killed your wife; you have killed your blessed baby and thrown it out the window; and you have outraged the laws of your country.

PUNCH: Nonsense, who told you that?

BEADLE: Never mind who told me; I shall take you up.

PUNCH: Then I shall knock you down. *(The beadle and Punch fight, and the beadle takes Punch away to prison.)*

◆

◀ *These Victorian Punch and Judy hand puppets are carved from wood and have cloth bodies. Punch came complete with a bean-bag stomach!*

Japanese Festival Dolls

Japanese girls display antique Festival Dolls on *O-hinamatsuri*, also known as Girl's Day. Every year on March 3 young girls are honored throughout Japan and each girl exhibits her dolls. This is the one day of the year devoted to honoring Japanese girls, and they are given special attention by their entire family, even by their brothers! Though many older customs and ways of thinking are rapidly changing in contemporary Japan, girls who own Festival Dolls often regard them as their most valued possessions. The dolls symbolize good health and fortune, and Japanese girls believe their spirits watch over them during the year.

The Japanese have celebrated Girl's Day for about three hundred years. The origin of the Festival comes from *nagashi-hina*, an ancient Shinto belief that a person could rid

1.

2.

3.

◄ **1** *These contemporary origami Japanese Festival Dolls represent the Emperor (top left), the Empress (top right), and three Ladies-in-Waiting. Their bodies are created by a series of folds using a single sheet of paper. Their crowns and utensils are cut from gold paper and show their position at Court. These paper dolls are traditionally made with blank faces.*
2 *This elaborate Japanese Festival Doll set is described as o-hinasama, a Japanese word used to denote special honor. The dolls represent the Court of the Fujiwara Period. The set includes the Emperor and Empress, Imperial attendants, and Court furniture and furnishings.*
3 *The Emperor is shown sitting on his throne and holding his ceremonial sword.*

The Empress — part of the Festival Doll set shown on page 21 — is wearing a richly brocaded kimono in the style of the Fujiwara Period. The doll is magnificently crafted in minute detail.

his body of evil spirits by breathing them into paper dolls and floating the dolls away on a stream. Later, clay dolls were also used and some were floated away while others were put on shelves for exhibit. In the 1700s the dolls evolved to represent figures in the twelfth-century Imperial Court, and the *hinaningyo,* as the dolls were called, were presented once a year on a seven-tiered stand.

Master craftsmen have made beautiful dolls of porcelain or carved ivory in elaborate ceremonial dress. They are so delicately designed that they have been handed down from mother to daughter through generations of a family. Some families have simpler or less expensive Festival Dolls that are made of clay, carved from wood, or made from folded paper. The heirloom dolls were often kept in small brick outdoor shelters constructed to protect valued possessions in the event the family house was destroyed by earthquake or fire. In spite of these shelters, many Festival Dolls were destroyed during the 1923 Tokyo earthquake and the World War II bombing of Japanese cities.

Many Japanese mothers nostalgically remember the Festival Dolls from their childhood and use the dolls to teach their children the social hierarchy of Imperial Japan and the etiquette of ancient court life. There are fifteen or more hinaningyo who represent the Imperial Court; each figure illustrates a particular person who is elaborately dressed and placed on a specially designed display stand. At the top sits the Emperor with his ornate crown, the Empress with her golden fan, and the delicate ladies-in-waiting who serve the royal couple. One lady-in-waiting carries a tiny ladle, another a gold *sake* pot, and the third a stand on which to place the sake. Lower on the display is an old man holding many scrolls, who represents civil law, and a young *samuri* warrior armed with swords and arrows. There are five court musicians with gongs and drums, and the Emperor's three attendants holding an umbrella, a silk package, and the Emperor's tiny pair of shoes. Black lacquered cabinets and tables, elaborate serving dishes, flower blossoms and lanterns complete the scene.

On O-hinamatsuri girls arrange their dolls, which have been carefully packed away for the entire year, to be displayed in the *tokonoma,* the place in the home for showing special and important objects. A set ritual is followed in unwrapping and exhibiting the dolls. First the girls assemble the display stand and cover it with red cloth. Then they put each doll in its designated place, symbolic of its position at Court. At the bottom of the stand the girls add their everyday play dolls so they will be able to enjoy the celebration as well. Girls wear their best *kimono* and invite friends to admire the Festival Dolls, eat red, green and white rice cakes called *mochi,* and play games.

Often girls play games and activities that are traditional on O-hinamatsuri. Two of these are *o-tedama* and *origami*. O-tedama is a game similar to jacks, but instead of using six-pointed pegs, the Japanese toss brightly colored bean bags. Origami is the art of folding paper to represent objects: birds, animals and figures. It is a favorite Japanese pastime. The folded paper Festival Dolls shown here, and the paper crane (called *tsuru*) which is a symbol of good fortune, are examples of traditional origami figures made on Girl's Day. Another game girls play is *mama-goto* or "like mama." They imitate their mothers by playing house and serve each other miniature cakes and tea. This is a special part of Girl's Day.

Department stores throughout Japan exhibit Festival Dolls each year, and elaborate sets of dolls are still sold, but many families no longer bother with the display and instead hang a scroll in their tokonoma with pictures of the dolls or purchase dolls in a glass case. These families no longer observe the old rituals involved in setting up the display. However, other Japanese families still honor the tradition and carefully assemble the display of Festival Dolls, which gracefully express the beauty, spirit and culture of Imperial Japan.

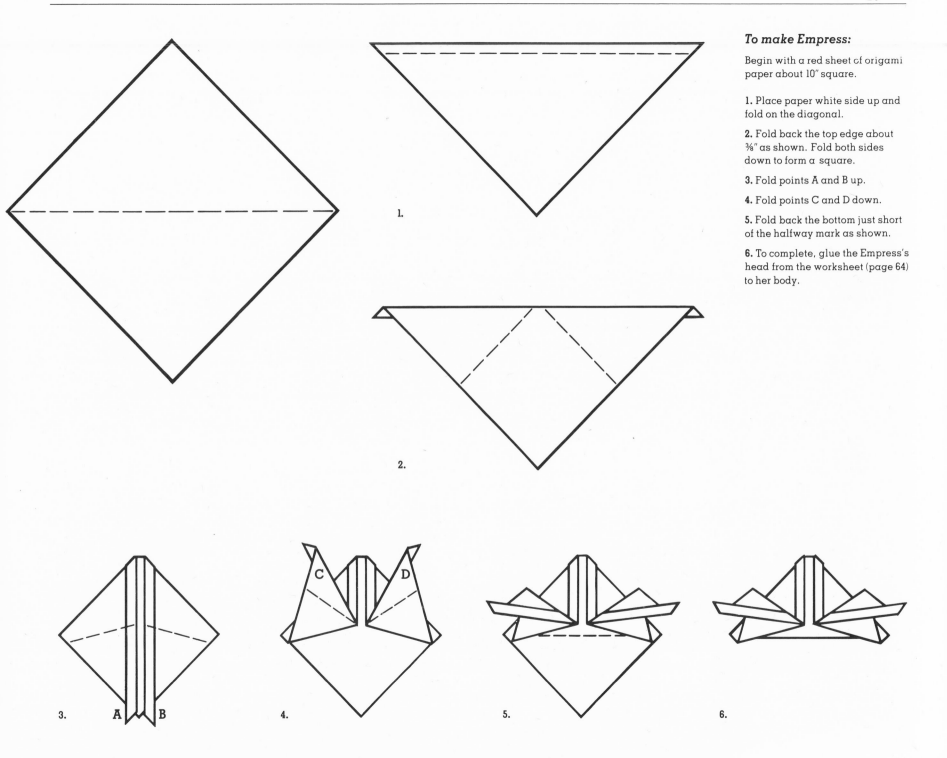

To make Empress:

Begin with a red sheet of origami paper about 10" square.

1. Place paper white side up and fold on the diagonal.

2. Fold back the top edge about ⅜" as shown. Fold both sides down to form a square.

3. Fold points A and B up.

4. Fold points C and D down.

5. Fold back the bottom just short of the halfway mark as shown.

6. To complete, glue the Empress's head from the worksheet (page 64) to her body.

To make the Emperor:

Begin with a red sheet of origami paper about 10" square.

1. Place paper white side up and fold on the diagonal.

Do the same with a purple origami sheet and place it folded underneath the red triangle. The folded sheets should be separate, not sandwiched.

Do the remaining folds with both sheets together, as if they were one sheet.

2. Fold both sides down so that the points overlap at the bottom, making sure that the top of the folds create a robe-like opening.

3. Fold points up, starting the fold where the pieces cross.

4. Take the red sheet of paper and fold down the red points, leaving the purple sheet as in step 3.

5. Next, fold the purple points down, but at a lesser angle so that the red points show.

6. Fold back the bottom triangle.

7. To complete, glue the Emperor head (from worksheet, page 64) to his body.

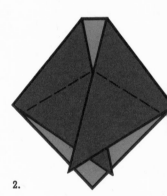

1.

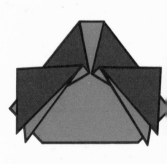

2.

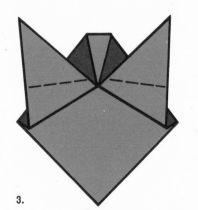

3.

4.

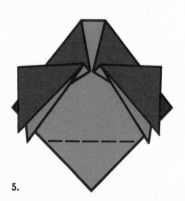

5.

6.

To make robes for the Ladies-in-Waiting:

Begin with a white sheet of paper about 9″ square.

1. Fold on the diagonal.

2. Fold sides down so the points meet at the bottom.

3. Taking only the top layer, fold the points up so they touch the top exactly.

4. Take point A and, allowing triangles to open, fold point A to point B. This is a difficult fold, but will work if you do it carefully. This fold creates a square on each side.

5. Fold back top of square at C, then fold tip up at D.

6. You need to make three robes, one for each Lady-in-Waiting.

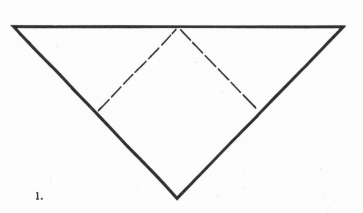

1.

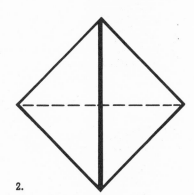

2.

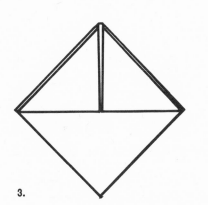

3.

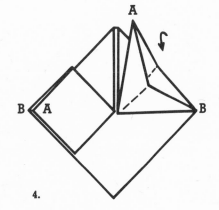

4.

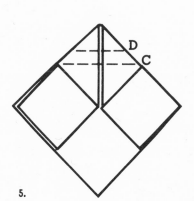

5.

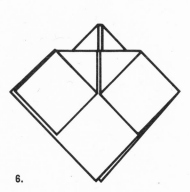

6.

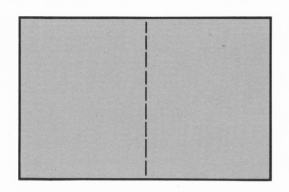

To make pleated dresses for the Ladies-in-Waiting:

Begin with a red sheet of origami paper 7¾" x 11".

1. Fold the long side of the sheet in half to mark the middle and unfold.

2. Make five accordian folds as shown, folding from left to center.

3. and **4.** Make four more overlapping accordian folds as shown, folding from right to center.

5. To make the dress for the middle Lady-in-Waiting shown in the photo on page 21, cut the sides of the dress straight as shown by the dotted lines.

6. To make the dresses of the left and right Ladies-in-Waiting in the photo on page 21, cut the sides of the dresses in a curve as shown by the dotted lines.

7. You need to make three robes, one for each Lady-in-Waiting.

8. To complete the Festival Dolls glue the heads from the worksheet (page 64) to the bodies you have folded.

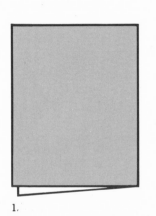

1.

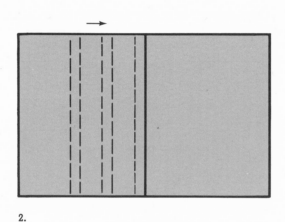

2.

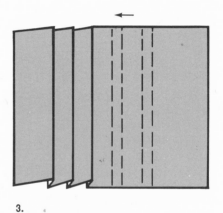

3.

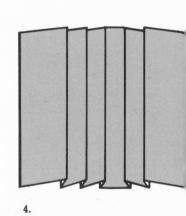

4.

5.

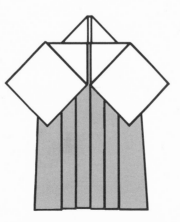

5a. Robe is shown glued in place.

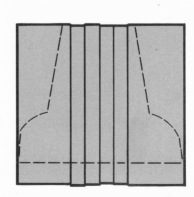

6.

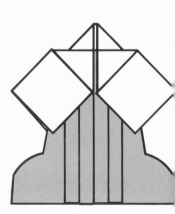

6a. Robe is shown glued in place.

The Brownies

In Scottish folklore, Brownies are tiny elf-like creatures who perform helpful deeds at night. People never see them, but their helpfulness is a reminder of their presence; they might sweep floors, clean pans, rescue crops, or in magical ways assist in childbirth. Scottish children believe that Brownies like small bowls of milk and cake set aside for them as gifts, but that this is the only reward they may accept. The Brownie Girl Scouts were named after these elves; they are supposed to demonstrate Brownie traits in their good deeds and thoughtfulness to others.

Palmer Cox was an illustrator of children's books and newspapers who worked in New York in the latter part of the 1800s. He enjoyed illustrating, but always hoped to devote more time to writing children's stories. As a boy growing up in a Scottish community in the province of Quebec, Cox had heard stories of the Brownies and decided to create his own version of these elves. His drawings first appeared in *St. Nicholas*, a children's magazine, and were so well liked that Cox decided in 1887 to write a book about them. He called it *The Brownies, Their Book*, and it set the style of prose and created the Brownie image that Cox used for all his later Brownie books. His stylized, elf-like characters had whimsical expressions, combining innocence with mischievousness, and they had rounded bodies with long skinny legs and pointed feet.

In his stories Cox adapted his Brownies to reflect some of the changes that were taking place in America at the turn of the century. Brownies imitated human activities — they went bicycling, visited the circus, and rode a horse and cart — all in a world much too large for them. Because the nineteenth century was a period of great immigration to the United States, Cox created Brownie immigrants — the Irishman, the Chinaman, the German, the Canadian, and the Dutchman. Cox also created the Brownie Policeman, Sailor, and Uncle Sam. Although many of these characters were stereotyped, Cox portrayed them with humor and warmth.

As the Brownies became successful they

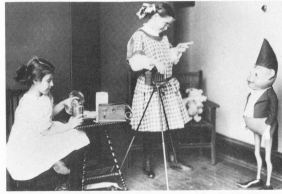

▲ *The Brownie camera was first manufactured by the Eastman Kodak company in 1900. Here is a 1908 photo of the No. 2 Folding Brownie. The girl on the left is mixing developing chemicals.*

How to make the Brownies (use worksheet on page 57)

1. Cut out Brownie head and body pieces from the worksheet page.

2. Fold Brownie body in half at the shoulders so that it stands up.

3. Insert the head into the hole in body from below and fold hands in front of the body to hold in place.

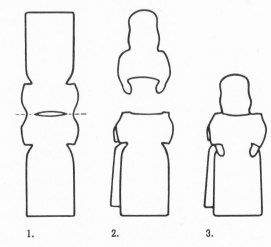

1.   2.   3.

◀ *A Palmer Cox illustration from St. Nicholas, an early children's magazine.*

were reproduced in many forms: as decorations on household objects and in cloth pattern dolls to be cut and sewn. They were even used in advertising. Some of the Brownies shown here were used to sell biscuits. Children could get a full set of sixteen stand-up paper Brownies by sending four two-cent stamps to the biscuit company. Their slogan was, "Test the Brownies in biscuits, and your pleasure will be complete. The proof of the Brownies is in the eating." The Eastman Kodak Company may have named the Brownie camera after them, or perhaps after its inventor Frank Brownell, or even after George Eastman's dog Brownie—no one really knows. In any event Kodak packaged the camera with an illustration of one of Cox's Brownies. The Brownies' appeal and popularity were so widespread that they became as universally recognized as Mickey Mouse would be to children fifty years later.

Palmer Cox became famous for his thirteen books, and his Brownies were reproduced everywhere. After two decades of bringing Brownie adventure stories to children, Cox returned to Canada, where children from all over the world sent him letters addressed to "Brownie Castle."

▶ *This label was pasted on wooden crates used to package oranges grown in California and shipped across the country. The Brownies were used to promote sales. In the 1940s wooden crates were replaced by printed cardboard cartons, making paper labels obsolete.*

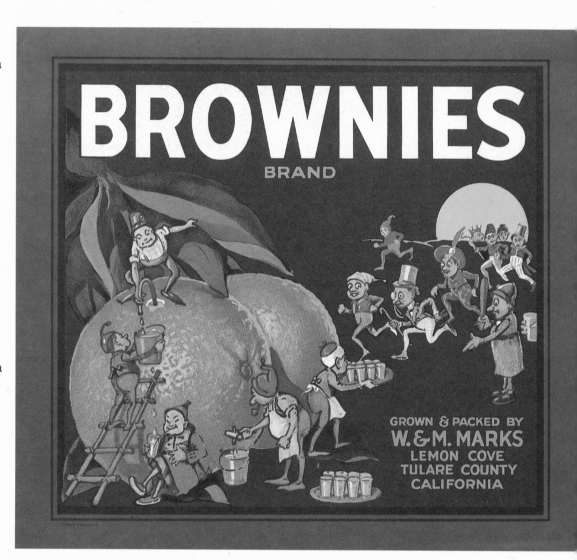

Folk-art Toys and Crafts

▲ *This Lazy Tongs doll has wooden levers, a cloth body, and a paper face and hands. Bells are attached to the hands. The printed face shows a young girl on one side and a man on the reverse!*

Before the twentieth century, folk-art toys and crafts were mostly handmade, principally by local craftspeople using familiar materials. The toys were simple, the origin of the parts and the purpose of the toys easy to understand. Likewise, crafts were simply made, their design evolving naturally from a clear and uncomplicated perception of decorative or functional needs. Today it is often difficult to understand how toys and crafts are made, for their manufacture and materials have become complicated and obscure. And, unlike the mass-produced toys of today, the folk-art toys and crafts of the past express the imagination and skill of each individual craftsman.

The crafts and toys in this section are easy to make, and they use materials that are easily available. After you have made some of them, perhaps you will design and make your own toys and crafts, and discover that this can be a lot more fun than buying them.

Lazy Tongs Toy

The Lazy Tongs toy consists of an interconnected series of levers that extend when the handle is squeezed. This principle is used in adjustable safety gates to close off stairs from young toddlers, in elevator doors that close for passenger safety, and was used in many common household items, such as extending gas lamps and telephones, in the early part of this century.

The principle of lazy tongs' construction was used in several different toys. In one toy, horses were attached to the levers; they would suddenly appear to gallop forward when the handle was squeezed and the levers extended. When the handle to this Lazy Tongs toy is squeezed, the doll grows four feet. The doll has the face of a pretty young Japanese girl on one side and the face of a grumpy old Japanese man on the reverse side. The toy originated in the United States but reflects the interest in Japanese culture, customs, and dress inspired by travelers to Japan in the late 1800s.

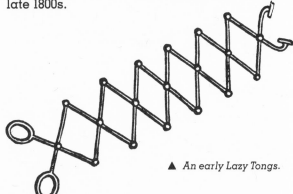

▲ *An early Lazy Tongs.*

► *These soldiers and cavalrymen are two of many ingenious Lazy Tongs toys.*

How to make a Lazy Tongs Toy (use worksheet on page 65)

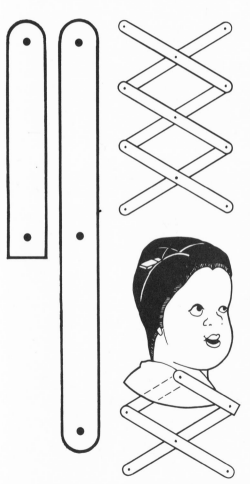

To make Lazy Tongs levers:

1. Using 4½"-long popsicle sticks, take twelve sticks and drill (or punch with nail and hammer) three holes into each stick. You may use the stick shown as a guide to make all your holes the same distance apart.

2. From your set of finished sticks, take two and cut them down to 2½".

3. Arrange sticks as shown in the drawing. Be sure that all the sticks going in one direction are above all the sticks going in the opposite direction.

4. Attach the sticks by threading string through the holes and knotting each, or attach with small paper fasteners. (This toy was originally made by peening or hammering over the point of a nail to attach the sticks.)

5. Cut out the head from the worksheet and attach as shown. Using the two smaller sticks, put one above the head, the other below.

6. To complete, pull the cloth body over the head and pull and knot the gathering thread around the neck.

To make cloth body for Lazy Tongs:

1. Begin with an 11" x 13" piece of cloth.

2. Fold ¼" for hem at top and bottom.

3. At ¼" from top of hem make gathering stitch. (Leave extra thread untied for assembly later.)

4. Fold cloth in half and stitch seam ¼" from end. (Cloth should be inside out.) Leave a 1" opening for the arm in the seam 2" from the top. On the other side cut a 1" opening 2" from the top for the other arm.

5. Turn cloth right side out.

To make arms for Lazy Tongs:

1. Begin with two pieces of cloth 2¾" x 2½".

2. Fold each cloth piece in half and stitch seam ¼" from edge. (Cloth should be inside out.)

3. Turn cloth right side out.

4. Cut out hands from the worksheet and glue them about ¼" into each arm sleeve.

5. Insert arms about ¼" into openings in cloth body and sew.

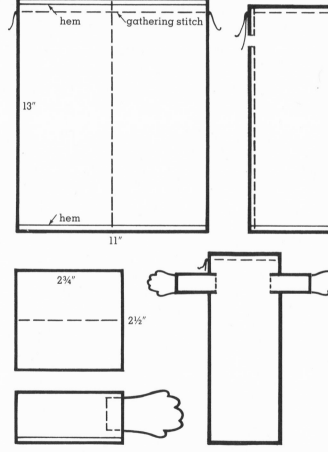

Wycinanki

▲ *This bold symmetrical Kurpie-style Wycinanki was made by folding a sheet of black paper three times and then cutting the pattern.*

Polish peasants often decorated their homes with paper patterns and designs which they pasted to their walls. The intricate patterns were cut out in the shapes of trees and flowers from the surrounding countryside and familiar farm animals and birds. During the long winter months Polish women spent evenings cutting out paper designs using their husbands' sheep-shearing scissors, a tool common to almost every farm family. They cut amazingly refined and delicate shapes with the tips of these blunt and heavy shears. The women decorated the upper walls, window panes and ceiling beams of their farm cottages with the paper cut-outs, which became an inexpensive way to create interesting interiors. These paper silhouettes were called *Wycinanki* (pronounced vee-chee-non-kee), and the designs and methods they used in making these paper cut-outs have become a traditional Polish folk-art.

Wycinanki originated about one hundred years ago. The first designs frequently used roosters and sometimes a spruce tree or lily motif. Later, without cameras to document special occasions, Polish women cut out scenes of weddings and family celebrations. The Wycinanki had become more than decoration; they were a means by which a family could record events and pass them on to their children. Easter became a favorite time for making new Wycinanki; the women did their spring cleaning, dusting everything and

whitewashing the walls to contrast with the brightly colored cut-outs.

Different regions of Poland developed their own unique styles of Wycinanki designs. The two best known are *Kurpie* (pronounced coor-pye) and *Lowicz* (pronounced wo-vitz). In the Kurpie district, single-color silhouettes, which are extremely bold, were made using the *leluji* (le-loo-ya) or lily, the *drzewka* (dz-heuka) or small tree (often called the Kurpie tree), and *zielka* (zh-yelka) or herbs. Women made these by folding a sheet of paper in half and cutting through both layers to create a symmetrical design.

The Lowicz district is famous for its multi-colored scenes of country life. These scenes, which the local people called *kodry*, were cut into long horizontal bands so the artist could include many figures in his design: a wedding party, a woman working at her spinning wheel, men harvesting, or a parade of peasants in brightly colored costumes. The artist cut each figure and decorative motif separately; colored concentric or overlaid shapes were glued upon each other, creating layers of colors. This method was used to illustrate the peasant folk-costumes of the Lowicz region in order to show the many stripes on men's pants and on women's blouses, jackets, kerchiefs, and boots. A *kodra* took many hours to make, and in this type of Wycinanki the designs were often intricate and detailed. The Lowicz artists are also

MAZOWSZE

known for their open-work circular designs and for the colorful ribbon patterns that are similar in shape to prize ribbons. The ribbons are among the oldest Wycinanki patterns and are still used in modern bridal wreath decorations.

The Kurpie-style and the Lowicz-style are easy to tell apart. The Lowicz-style is multi-colored and very decorative. The designs are intricate, with many layers of colored paper. They are less abstract and have a more

◀ *On the left are colorful Lowicz-style Wycinanki used to decorate greeting cards. On the right is a bold Kurpie-style cut-out of a tree, roosters and birds. Mazowsze is a large region of Poland. (Kurpie Wycinanki courtesy of the Polish Embassy.)*

contained quality than the highly graphic single-color Kurpie-style.

The popularity of Wycinanki continued in the early part of the twentieth-century but began to decline as the Polish people were disrupted by war, politics, and urbanization. But in the last twenty years the Polish government has sponsored Wycinanki contests and classes to revive this craft and educate people about this unique art form. Contemporary artists have added the dove as the symbol of peace to their designs. Many Polish Americans and Poles living in other countries are interested in maintaining their cultural heritage, and they continue to make Wycinanki and to display them in their homes.

How to make Wycinanki (use worksheet on page 72)

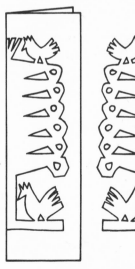

To make a Kurpie-style Wycinanki:

1. Fold a sheet of paper in half and draw a picture or design bordering on the fold.

2. Cut out the picture, cutting through both layers to create a symmetrical design.

To make a Lowicz-style Wycinanki:

1. Draw a picture on a sheet of paper and add overlaying shapes to the design.

2. Trace the shapes on different colors of paper and cut out each shape.

3. Glue down the bottom shapes first and add the overlapping shapes to your design.

Indian Birchbark Boxes

▲ *This berry bucket was made from one large piece of birchbark which was folded and then sewn together with spruce root.*

Before the encroachment of European settlers, American Indians lived in harmony with and dependence on nature. These Native Americans used the natural resources around them to construct their shelters, make their clothes, and supply their food. The Passamaquoddy Indians, living in the woodlands of Maine, were particularly dependent on the birch forests. They devised a multitude of ways to use birchbark, carefully removing the outer bark so as not to harm the cambium layer growing beneath. They built birchbark canoes, used birchbark to cover their wigwams, and made birchbark berry baskets and buckets, maple sugar sap kettles, cups, pails, and boxes. They created baby cradles, drums and children's dolls from this deciduous tree, and when caught in a sudden downpour they even made temporary rain jackets with the waterproof bark.

These Indians scratched floral patterns, geometric designs, maps, and pictographs into the bark. They made pictographs to record special events, show scenes from everyday life, or illustrate characters from Indian mythology. To make birchbark containers they cut new winter bark, which is heavier than summer bark, and turned it over so that they could scratch or cut into the softer inner surface with a sharp bone or knife, exposing the lighter layer beneath. This created a light line drawing on a dark background. Or sometimes they scratched away the background, creating the relief effect of a dark image on a light ground.

Birchbark was so important in these Native Americans' daily lives that the birch came to figure in their myths and legends, which were passed from generation to generation in the oral tradition of poems and songs. They believed that *Glooscap*, the first person on earth and the greatest spirit who endowed all things with life, commanded the birch to take care of and provide for them. Passamaquoddy legends are filled with supernatural spirits, and the Passamaquoddy and many other Indian tribes believed that in mythological times animals acted as humans and humans were likewise able to take the form of animals. Owls, rabbits, porcupines, wolves, badgers, wildcats, otters, beavers, and bears inhabit these numerous tales. The legends represent Indian religious beliefs and mythological history, but they are also filled with humor and lessons in common sense.

Tomah Joseph was a governor of the Passamaquoddy people at Peter Dana's Point Reservation near Calais, Maine, in 1885. He was a hunting and fishing guide for President Franklin Roosevelt when Roosevelt was a young man at Campobello Island. Tomah was not only a political leader of his people, but also a craftsman and artist. He made birchbark boxes which he decorated with mythological animals and figures taken from Passamaquoddy legends and with scenes from everyday life. Tomah drew the wildcat *Loup-Cervier*, the rabbit *Mahtigwess,* and the owl *Koko-gus* on the birchbark box shown here. The animals Tomah illustrated are characters in the Passamaquoddy legend told on this page. Interestingly, the white man's culture has affected this story as it has been told and retold through generations of Indians. Over time a church and preacher and a ship and captain appear as elements in the story, reflecting continuing changes and influences on Indian life.

In the legend of Wildcat and Rabbit, Rabbit plays the trickster — a role that appears frequently in all Indian mythology. Here Rabbit embodies the spirit of the mighty Glooscap who always outsmarts his enemies by strategy and cunning and by using his *m'teoulin* or magic power. In this story Rabbit tricks Wildcat with his magic power and avoids becoming Wildcat's dinner.

The legend of Wildcat and Rabbit was told by Tomah Joseph to Charles G. Leland who recorded it in *The Algonquin Legends of New England,* published by Houghton, Mifflin and Company, 1884. Reissued by Singing Tree Press, 1968.

How Rabbit became wise by being original, and of the terrible magic he played on Loup-Cervier, the wicked wildcat.

Rabbit had trouble deciding what he should be. He had tried to be like the otter, but he could not swim. By copying the woodpecker he only hurt his nose pecking at trees. When he tried to imitate the bear, he was even more hopeless. Then he hit upon something he was good at which was original and much better than trying to copy other animals. Rabbit applied himself to the study of m'teoulin, or magic, and in time became so successful that he could make crops suddenly appear, cause an awful storm, and sometimes even raise ghosts from the dead. His great perseverance and stubbornness finally paid off.

Now the rabbit is the natural prey of Loup-Cervier, or Wildcat, and in our story Rabbit becomes the object of Wildcat's dinner. But in this legend Rabbit outsmarts Wildcat by making use of his magic powers.

One day Wildcat stealthily approached Rabbit's wigwam. Rabbit was obliged to use

all his m'teoulin powers to escape. He picked up a handful of wood chips and threw one as far as he could and, using his magical wits, he took a long jump and landed on the chip. He threw another and landed on it again, and continued this until he had gone a great distance and then he ran away as fast as he could. He did this in order not to leave tracks or scent. When Wildcat arrived at Rabbit's wigwam he found him gone, and in great anger Wildcat circled the wigwam round and round in widening circles until he finally discovered Rabbit's tracks. Wildcat chased poor Rabbit until nightfall, and Rabbit had barely enough time "to trample down the snow a little, and stick up a spruce twig on end and sit on it."

When Wildcat caught up to Rabbit he found an old man, very dignified, with gray hair and long ears, sitting in a wigwam. He asked the old man if he had seen a rabbit run by; the old man replied that of course he had seen dozens of rabbits run by all day and invited the weary Wildcat to stay for dinner. After a fine supper Wildcat was content to sleep and after so much effort, he didn't wake until morning. To his surprise he found himself lying

How to make an Indian Birchbark Bucket (use worksheet on page 73)

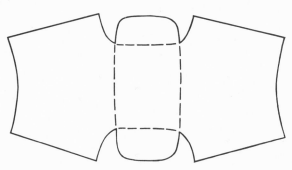

1. Cut out pattern from worksheet page.

2. Fold along dotted lines, first folding in the small flaps, then the larger sides of the bucket.

3. Tape or stitch the berry bucket together.

4. To make a handle, run string through the holes at the top of the bucket and tie a knot in each end as shown.

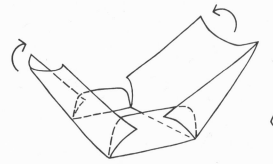

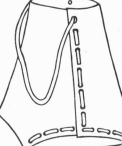

in the snow, cold and hungry. Wildcat suddenly realized that he had been fooled by Rabbit, and all that had happened the night before was only a grand illusion. With extreme rage Wildcat took up the chase again. He ran after Rabbit all day and, when night came, again caught up to him.

But Rabbit, with more time to work his magic, had prepared an even greater illusion. He again trampled down the snow but this time made a great clearing and threw down many branches. These became people populating an entire Indian village. The first building Wildcat saw was a church and, peering in, he asked if a rabbit had been seen running by. He was asked to enter; when he had come in he was forced to listen to a long sermon. He heard an old preacher with long pointed ears speak on the subject of wickedness and vindictiveness, but Wildcat didn't care for the sermon and hardly listened. When it was over he again asked his question. And again he was told that many rabbits run by all day, but that perhaps the Chief of the village could answer his question. The elderly Chief was a remarkable-looking gentleman with long pointed locks that stood up in a most unusual way. The Chief kindly invited Wildcat to dinner with him. After dinner, Wildcat was asked to spend the night and was given a soft bearskin to sleep on. He was very happy. However, when he awoke he was miserable. He found himself lying in a swamp, cold and terribly hungry.

But worst of all he knew he had been tricked and humiliated again. He hated Rabbit even more. He sprang up and again pursued his prey. He ran all day and by nightfall approached another village. This time he was so exhausted he gasped, "Have—you—seen—a—Rab—bit run this way?" The people, seeing how weary he was, treated him with kindness and felt pity for such a bedraggled figure. Some cried in sympathy for Wildcat's suffering and they begged him to stay with them. There was a grand feast and the Chief, who had two long feathers on his head, asked the wildcat for a song. Wildcat's song was filled with hatred and mocking for rabbits. When he was finished he asked the Chief to sing a song; the Chief consented but said everyone must shut their eyes to hear his song. Then Chief Rabbit drew his *timheyen* or tomahawk and with it gave Wildcat a tremendous thwack. When Wildcat recovered enough to stand, he found himself deep in snow, cold and hungry, his head bleeding from the dreadful blow.

Hardly able to walk, poor Wildcat wandered on until he came to an old man and his daughter. At the sight of the wounded wildcat, the old man became so concerned that he went for a doctor. Now the doctor was an old man and had two horn-like shapes on his head, and Wildcat, becoming suspicious, asked the doctor where he got his split nose and why the soles of his feet were so yellow. The doctor said that a chip of stone split his nose when he was hammering wampum beads, and that the tobacco he had stood in made his soles yellow. Wildcat was relieved and his suspicions were allayed as the doctor applied a cool salve to his wound. He was given wine and biscuits, and he rested in peace and soon fell asleep. But how wretched he became upon awakening! The cool salve was really hemlock needles and pine splinters which made his wound much more painful. After this latest disgrace, Wildcat swore to get his revenge.

Now Mahtigwess the Rabbit had almost come to the end of his m'teoulin, or magic power, in outsmarting Wildcat and he decided on one last effort to discourage Wildcat from ever pursuing him for his dinner again. Using all his magical abilities, he threw a chip far into a lake, and this chip seemed to change into a great ship that white men use. The ship had sails and flags that fluttered in the wind, and on the deck stood a stately gray-haired captain wearing a cocked hat with two long points. When Wildcat saw him he would not be fooled; diving into the water he swam toward the captain crying, "You cannot escape me this time Rabbit! I have you now!" And the captain, seeing the wildcat, ordered his crew to fire their muskets at this curious and vengeful figure. At that same moment, a group of nighthawks flying above swooped down, and all together made a sudden cry which sounded very much like a shot. Appalled, Wildcat felt he had really made an awful mistake this time and, turning in panic, he headed for shore. He was last seen running into the forest and no one knows what became of him, but some think that he is running there still.

▼ *The wildcat* Loup-Cervier, *the rabbit* Mahtigwess, *and the owl* Koko-gus, *three figures from Passamaquoddy legends, were drawn by Tomah Joseph on this birchbark box.*

Tongue-cut Sparrow

The Tongue-cut Sparrow, or *shita-kiri suzume* is an old Japanese folktale that demonstrates kindness rewarded and evil punished. It is a favorite fairy tale among Japanese children and is illustrated on picture cards that are used as a story-telling device. The small figures and magic lantern slides show other ways in which the popular subjects of this story have been reproduced. In Japan, the sparrow is a symbol of gracefulness.

Tongue-cut Sparrow Cards (use worksheets on pages 76-77)

▼ *The old man and the Tongue-cut Sparrow were very carefully made. Notice the tiny lines on the sparrow's face and the bushy eyebrows on the old man. He is about 5" tall.*

The story of the Tongue-cut Sparrow is about a kind old man who had a mean wife with a terrible temper. The old man made a pet of a tiny sparrow that flew near his house, and he fed and cared for him. He called him *Bidori*, meaning beauty-bird. One day when the old man was out working, his wife mixed some starch which she used for washing clothes. The sparrow ate some of the starch, which made the wife so angry that she cut off the sparrow's tongue and the sparrow flew away. When the old man learned what had happened he was very sorry and went to find Bidori.

He searched in the woods for some time, and finally the sparrow called to the old man and invited him to be a guest in his home. The sparrow was dressed in beautiful clothes and spoke in a human voice. The old man knew that sparrows don't have voices and realized that his pet must be a very special sparrow. Bidori lived in a beautiful house. The sparrow and his family served up a feast and entertained the old man by performing the *suzume ordori* or sparrow dance. The old man enjoyed himself, but when he realized it was getting late and his wife would worry he told the sparrow he must leave. The kindly sparrow then showed him two baskets. One was big and heavy and the other small and light; the sparrow told him to choose the one he would like to take as a present. The baskets were covered so the old man did not know what they contained, but he chose the lighter

of the two because he did not want to be greedy and he had to travel a long way home. When the old man returned home he told his wife what had happened and they opened th basket. It was filled with wonderful things— gold and silver, rolls of fine silk, and lots of coins. It was more than enough to make them rich for the rest of their lives!

However, the wife wondered about her husband's story and thought that if he had taken the larger basket they would have had even more; she decided to go back to the sparrow's house to try to get the other basket. When she reached the house she told the sparrow how glad she was to see him, and he offered her some tea. Bidori then brought out two baskets, one large and heavy, the other small and light, and told the wife to choose the one she wanted. The old woman quickly picked the larger one and hurried home, but the basket was so heavy that she stopped to rest. Then she decided to open the basket. Suddenly horrible things sprang up at her! There were snakes and demons an scary things and goblins that tried to grab he The old woman was terrified and ran home. When she arrived home she was very happy to see her husband and told him about the horrible things in the basket. Then she told him that she would never be greedy again. After that the old woman was always kind to everyone and was especially careful to feed the birds that flew into their garden.

Noah's Ark

In the Biblical story of Noah and the Flood, God spoke to Noah, commanding him to build an ark. Two beasts of every kind upon the earth, in addition to Noah and his family, were to go into the ark. Then rains fell for forty days and forty nights, causing a great flood which destroyed the world. Only those inside the ark survived.

This Old Testament story of Noah was the inspiration for the Noah's Ark toy. The traditional design of this wooden boat had a box-like superstructure with roof or sides which slide open to reveal pairs of carefully carved animals huddled within. Some arks contained as many as seventy-five pairs of animals.

Noah's Ark was a popular "Sunday Toy" in strict Puritan households, where hard work and piety were glorified and the wickedness of fun and idle play denounced. The Puritans set Sunday aside for prayer and Bible reading, but allowed children to bring out the ark, line up the animals two-by-two, and recount the story of Noah and the great Flood.

This traditional folk toy probably originated in the late 1500s in Oberammergau, Germany — now famous for its Easter Passion Plays. Oberammergau craftsmen produced so many toys that their remote area became

◀ *This colorful wooden Noah's Ark was made in the United States around the turn of the century. It originally had twenty pairs of animals.*

How to make Noah's Ark (use worksheets on pages 68-69)

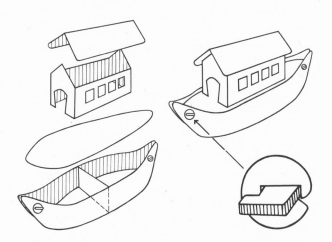

1. Cut out the pieces of the ark from the worksheets and assemble as shown. Use the locking pieces to fasten the ark together.

2. Cut out the animals and glue them to cardboard. To make the animals stand up:
Cut a slit in a piece of balsa wood and insert cardboard animal...

or tape animal to an opened paper clip...
or make tabs to tape to the animals' legs.

Papeles Cortados

▲ *Turned wooden ring used to make Noah's Ark animals.*

known as the Toy Valley. When they were snowed in during the winter, the valley craftsmen cooperated in a cottage industry: the toys were brought to each turner, finisher, and painter in sequence. Each added his touch to the toys as they progressed from house to house on their road to completion.

In the summer when the passes opened, merchants arrived to collect the finished toys. These merchants traveled in caravans to the various fairs that were held across the continent from England and France to Russia. The fairs, commemorating saints' days, hummed with activity as peddlers from all over Europe sold their toys. St. Bartholomew's Fair in England became the most famous of these fairs and was held annually for over seven hundred years from 1133 until 1855.

In 1814 the demand for Noah's Ark motivated craftsmen to devise a method to make the production of animals easier. A circular wooden ring with a cross section in the form of a particular animal was turned on a lathe. This process created the animal's basic shape; the craftsman then cut the ring into segments which were carved and sanded, giving each animal the appearance of a hand-crafted piece. This method of mass production represents a significant step in the transformation of a folk art into an industry.

Between 1825 and 1875 arks were made in many places in Europe and America. Pennsylvania and New England became important craft centers for toy production in the United States, and long before the advent of toy stores Noah's Arks were sold by peddlers going door to door. The craftsmen of Saxony in Germany made particularly beautiful arks which were brightly painted and detailed with doors, windows, porches, and decorative patterns; a dove holding an olive branch in its beak was often painted on the roof. Toy connoisseurs call this period of ark production in Saxony the "Great Period" of Noah's Arks.

▼ *A drawing of Noah's Ark, after a fifteenth century woodcut.*

Mexico is a country of fiestas! Religious and secular holidays occur throughout the year, and Mexicans celebrate both somber and joyous holidays with parades, feasts, and dancing. For these holidays Mexican craftsmen make a myriad of colorful folk-art figures and decorations, which are a blend of both Indian and Spanish influences.

Mexican artists are known for their papier mâché animals and people, their clay Trees of Life — filled with birds, flowers, berries, and figures — and their jewelry, pottery, and weaving. Certain folk-art objects are indigenous to particular parts of Mexico. Their styles and designs are often passed down through generations of a family. All Mexican folk-art combines remarkable boldness and vitality, joy and fantasy.

Among the most interesting folk-arts are the *papeles cortadoes*, or tissue paper cutouts. These cut-outs are used to decorate church altars, are strung as parade banners, and are used to decorate homes as well.

Craftsmen use many subjects for their paper cut-outs. One cut-out shows a dashing Lothario sporting a sombrero and serenading his lady while seated — improbably — on a galloping horse! A wedding cut-out is patterned with doves and bells. A Christmas stencil has a nativity scene with the Three Wise Men. Paper cut-outs of skeletons are made for All Soul's Day on November 2, known in Mexico as the Day of the Dead.

These skeletons are frequently funny: They are shown eating, drinking, dancing, laughing, and even riding ferris wheels. They are similar to Halloween skeletons in the United States. Some paper cut-outs have geometric patterns or floral designs with birds and angels. When these designs are cut from a large enough sheet of tissue paper they are used as tableclothes. In other Latin American countries cut-outs are used to stencil designs onto windows opening on the street. The stencil is held against the pane and a rag dipped in paint is patted over the cut-out. The resulting designs provide privacy as well as decoration.

To make papeles cortados the artist first draws a picture on a sheet of heavy paper about 20″ high by 30″ wide. He then puts his sketch on top of a stack of thirty or more sheets of colored paper. The stack is held in place with rows of pins placed along the edges. The craftsman pounds sharp knife blades through the layers of colored paper. When he is finished cutting out his design, he must be careful to separate the fragile sheets of tissue paper without tearing them. Figures of ani-

▲ *This nativity scene shows a shepherd in a sombrero, with a cactus in the background!*
▶ *St. George killing the dragon.*

mals, people, and flowers are often silhouetted by an adjacent abstract or geometric pattern creating a lace-like intricacy. A decorative panel sometimes runs along the bottom of the sheet.

Because these tissue paper cut-outs are fragile they are made for temporary use and are soon thrown away. But new ones are always made for the next fiesta.

How to make a Mexican Paper Cutout (use worksheet on page 80)

1. Cut out stencil from worksheet page.

2. Fold a sheet of tissue paper 29½″ long in half. Then accordian fold into four equal parts.

3. Place stencil on top of folded tissue paper and cut through the stencil into all the layers of tissue paper.

4. Open tissue paper and tape design on wall or to a window pane.

Bibliography

Toys

Fraser, Antonia. *A History of Toys*. New York: Delacorte Press, 1966.

McClintock, Marshall and Inez. *Toys in America*. Washington, D. C.: Public Affairs Press, 1961.

Moving Picture Toys

Macgowan, Kenneth. *Behind the Screen: The History and Techniques of the Motion Picture*. New York: Dell, 1965.

Wentz, Budd. *Paper Movie Machines*. San Francisco: Troubador Press, 1975.

Chinese Shadow Puppets

Barondes, R. de Rohan. *China: Lore, Legend and Lyrics*. New York: Philosophical Library, 1960.

Blackham, Olive. *Shadow Puppets*. London: Barrie and Rockliff, 1960.

Mills, Winifred H., and Louise M. Dunn. *Shadow Plays and How to Produce Them*. New York: Doubleday, Doran, 1938.

Simmen, René. *The World of Puppets*. New York: Thomas Y. Crowell, 1975.

Wimsatt, Genevieve. *Chinese Shadow Shows*. Cambridge, Mass.: Harvard University Press, 1936.

Pantins

Singleton, Easter. *Dolls*. New York: Payson and Clarke, 1927.

Punch and Judy

Baird, Bil. *The Art of the Puppet*. New York: Macmillan, 1965.

McPharlin, Paul. *The Puppet Theatre in America*. Boston: Plays, 1969.

Speaight, George. *Punch and Judy: A History*. Boston: Plays, 1970.

Japanese Festival Dolls

Ishii, Momoko. *The Dolls' Day for Yoshiko*. New York: Follett, 1966.

The Brownies

Fox, Carl. *The Doll*. New York: Harry N. Abrams, 1973.

Noah's Ark

Foley, Dan. *Toys Through the Ages*. New York: Chilton Books, 1962.

Tongue-cut Sparrow

Barbanson, Adrienne. *Fables in Ivory: Japanese Netsuke and Their Legends*. Rutland, Vt.: Charles E. Tuttle, 1961.

Milford, A. B. (Lord Redesdale). *Tales of Old Japan*. Rutland, Vt.: Charles E. Tuttle, 1966.

Sakada, Florence, ed. *Peach Boy and Other Japanese Children's Favorite Stories*. Rutland, Vt,: Charles E. Tuttle, 1958.

Seki, Keigo, ed. *Folktales of Japan*. Chicago: University of Chicago Press, 1963.

Native American Birchbark Box

Butler, Eva L., and Wendell S. Hadlock. *Uses of Birch-bark in the Northeast*. Robert Abbe Museum, Bulletin 7, 1957.

Leland, Charles G. *The Algonquian Legends of New England or Myths and Folk Lore of the Micmac, Passamaquoddy, and Penobscot Tribes*. Boston: Houghton, Mifflin, 1884.

Speck, Frank. "Penobscot Tales and Religious Beliefs." *Journal of American Folk-lore*, Vol. 48, No. 187, 1935.

Wycinanki

Gacek, Anna Zajac, ed. *Wycinanki: Polish Folk Paper-Cuts*. New Bedford, Mass.: Sarmatia Publications, 1972.

Jablonski, Romona. *The Paper Cut-Out Design Book*. Owings Mills, Md.: Stemmer House, 1976.

Jackowski, Aleksander, and Jadwiga Jarnuszkiewicz. *Folk Art of Poland*. Warsaw: Arkady, 1968.

Mexican Paper Cutouts

Moseley, Spencer, Pauline Johnson, and Hazel Koenig. *Crafts Design*. Belmont, Calif.: Wadsworth, 1962.

Sayer, Chloe. *Crafts of Mexico*. New York: Doubleday, 1977.

Temko, Florence. *Paper-Folded-Cut-Sculpted*. New York: Macmillan, 1974.

Cut out worksheet from this side. Cut out viewing slits.

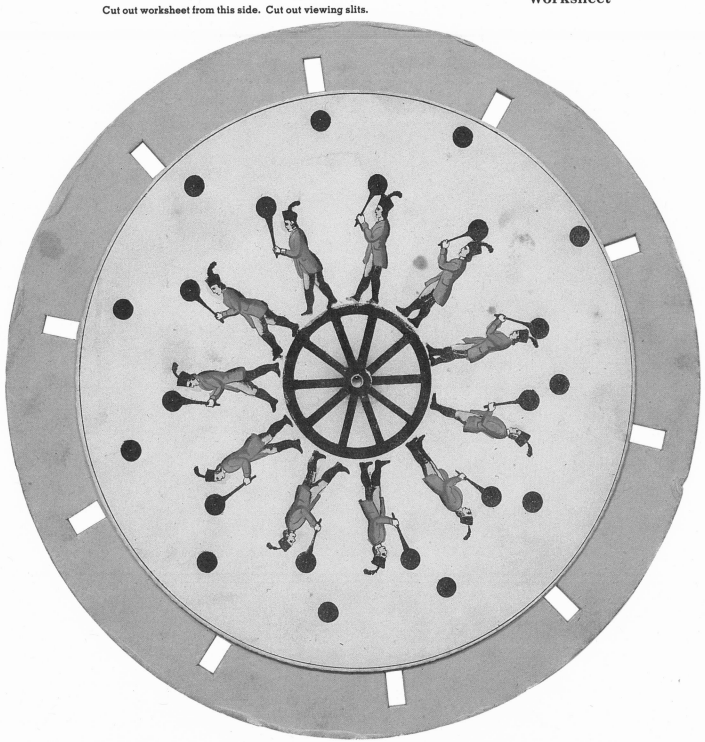

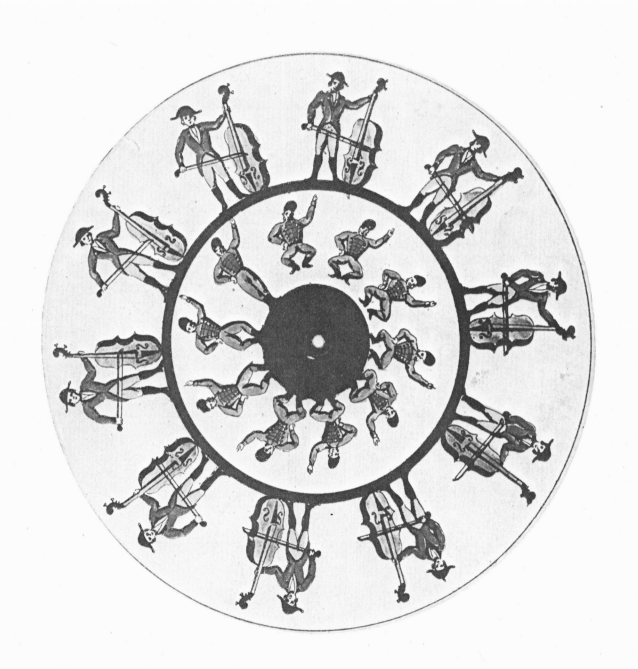

ARRANGED FOR THE ZOETROPE, PHOTOGRAPHED FROM THE LIFE IN 1878-79.

WALTZING NO.4 SERIES.A.

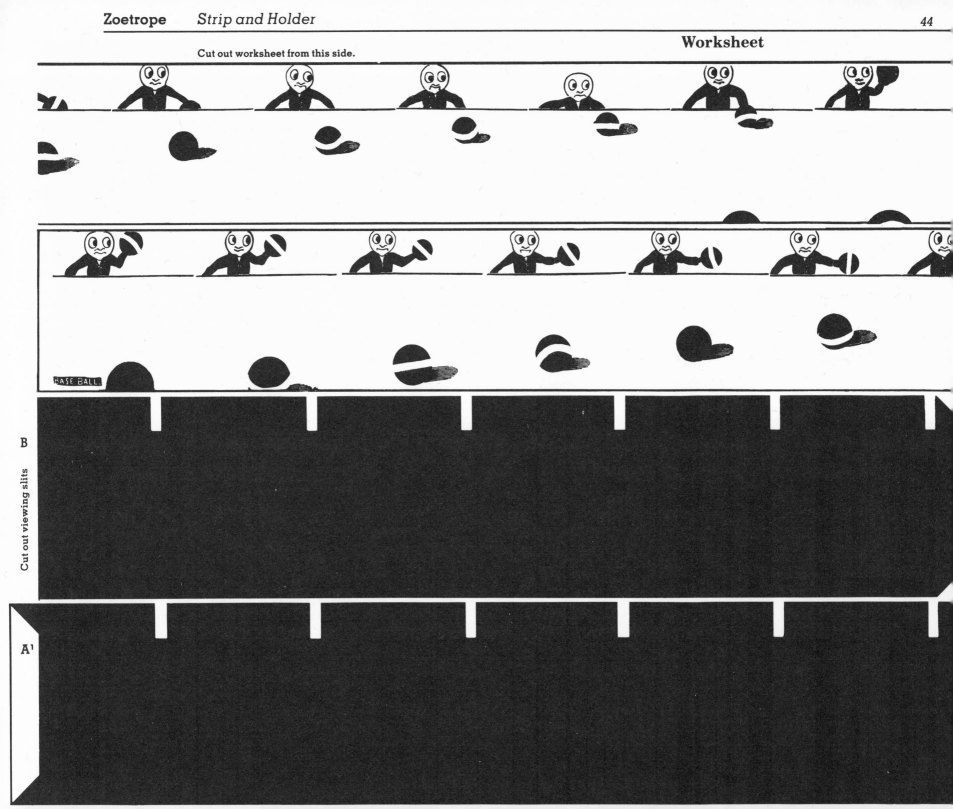

BASE BALL.

B

A¹

Cut out worksheet from this side.

Cut out worksheet from this side.

Worksheet

Worksheet

Cut out worksheet from this side.

1 The Star Spirit, Lao Hsiao Hsing, head of the Eight Immortals. 2 Maid Servant. 3 The Emperor, with pearls in his headdress. 4 The Monk, Tsuan Tsung. 5 Fighting Servant. 6 Spirit of the White Snake.

1

2

3

4

5

6

Emperor

Maid Servant

Star Spirit

White Snake
Spirit

Fighting
Servant

Monk

F

G H

E

E

Peasant or
Fisherman

D

G H

C

A

D

A

A

F

C B

B

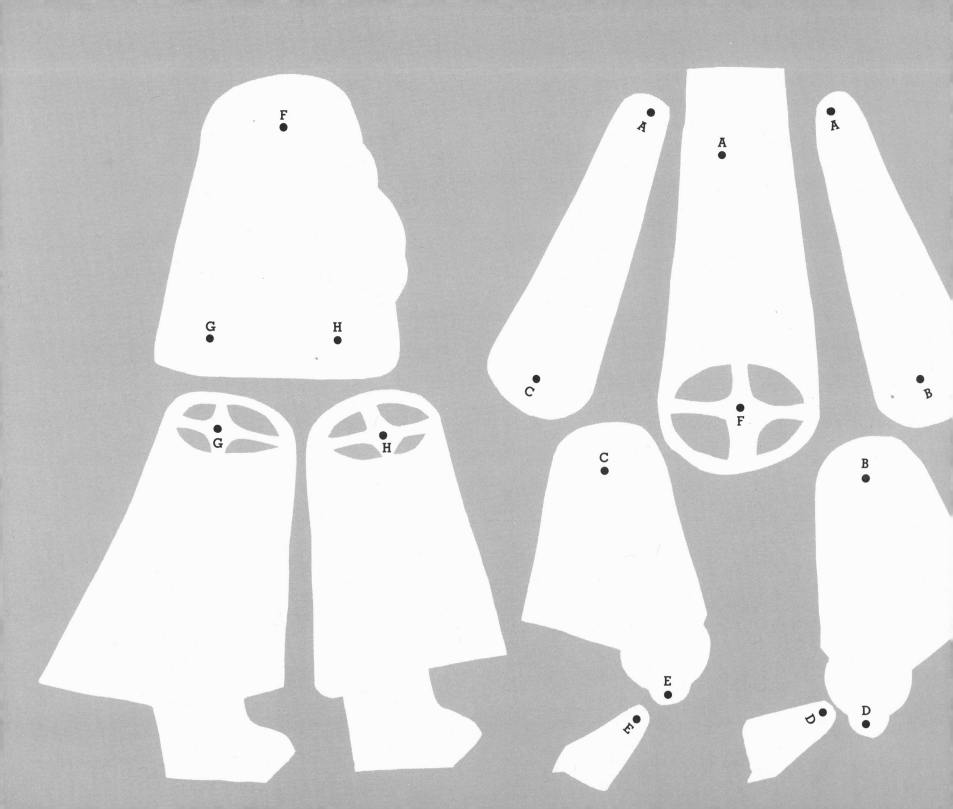

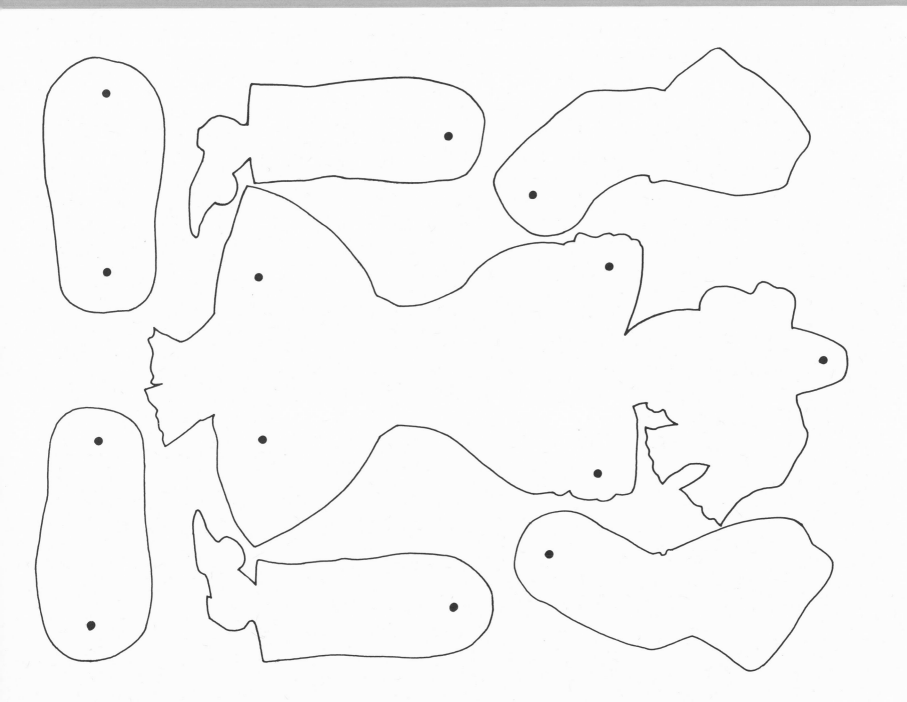

Cut out worksheet from this side.

IMAGERIE D'ÉPINAL, N° 1346

PIERRETTE. (Pantin).

IMAGERIE PELLERIN

Worksheet

Cut out worksheet from this side.

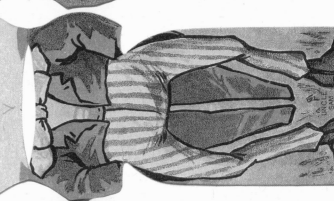

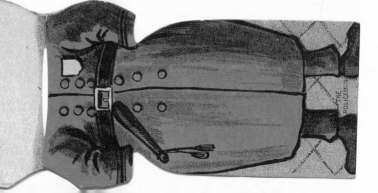

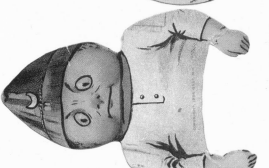

THE
NEW YORK
BISCUIT CO'S
BROWNIES

THE LATEST NOVELTY
IN
BISCUITS.

3NK 70-405

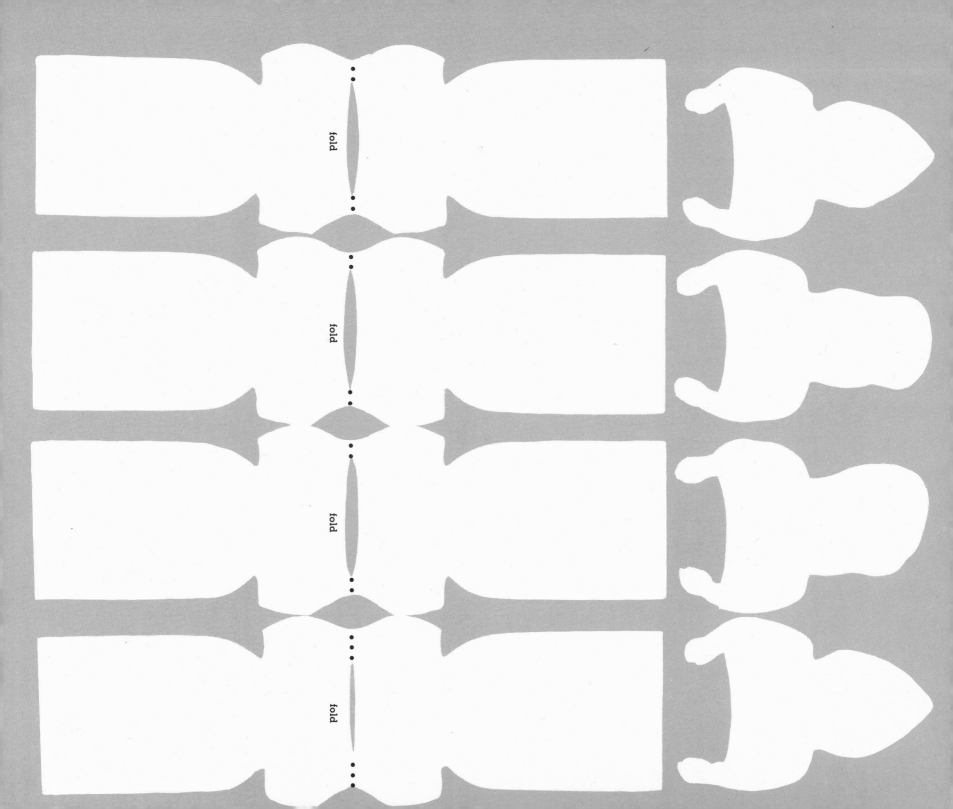

fold

fold

fold

fold

Cut out slit

Cut out slit

Cut out worksheet from this side.

Toby

Punch

Baby

Judy

Beadle

Cut out worksheet from this side.

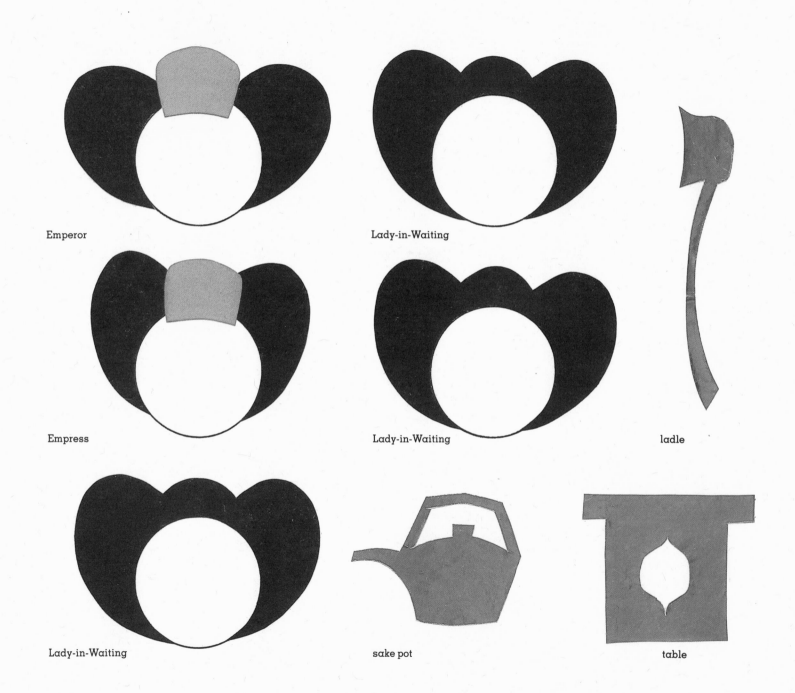

Emperor

Lady-in-Waiting

Empress

Lady-in-Waiting

ladle

Lady-in-Waiting

sake pot

table

Worksheet

Cut out worksheet from this side.

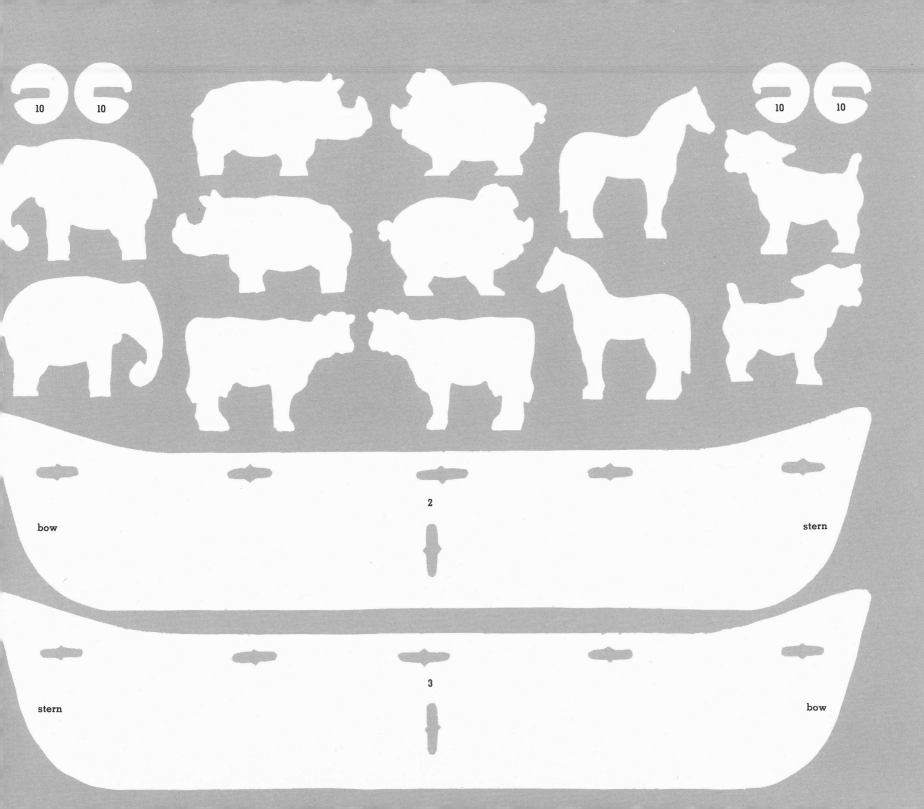

Cut out worksheet from this side.

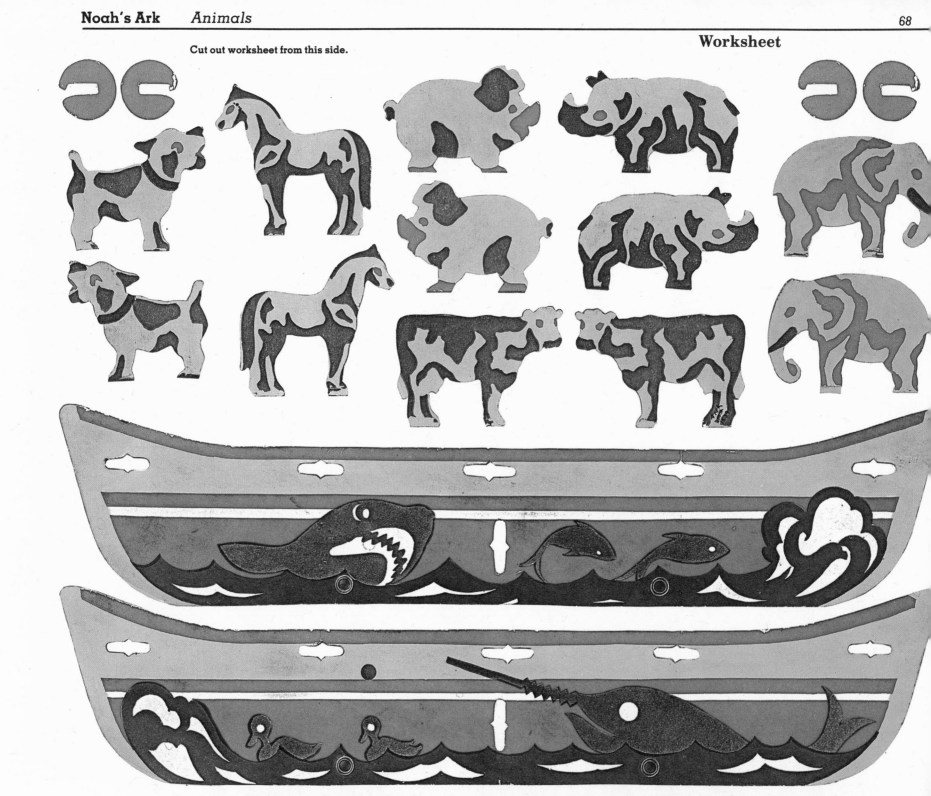

Cut out worksheet from this side.

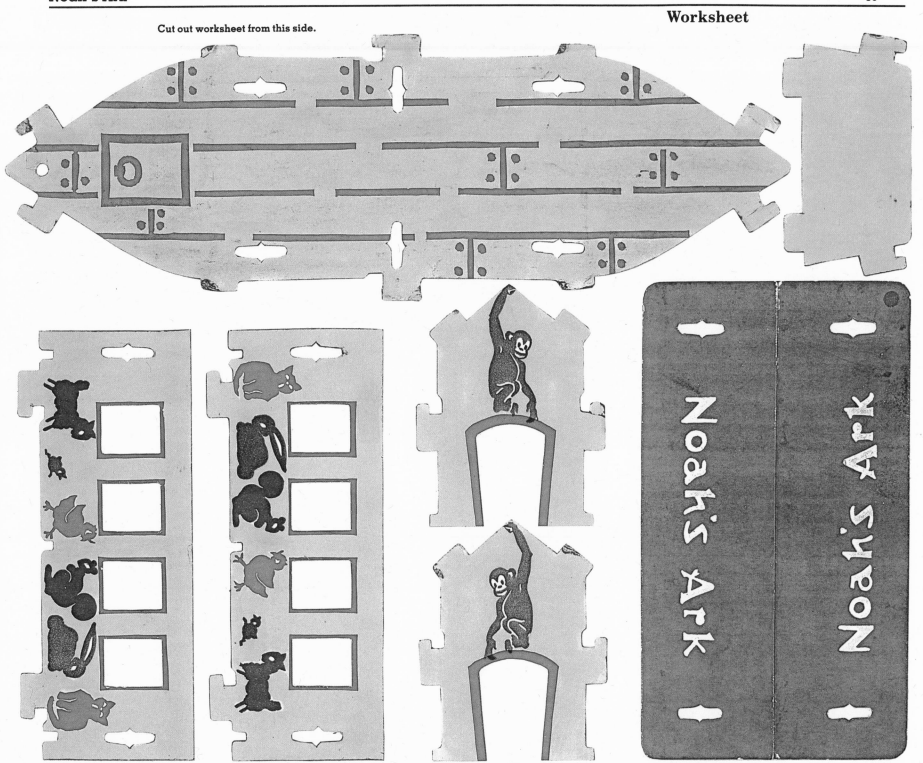

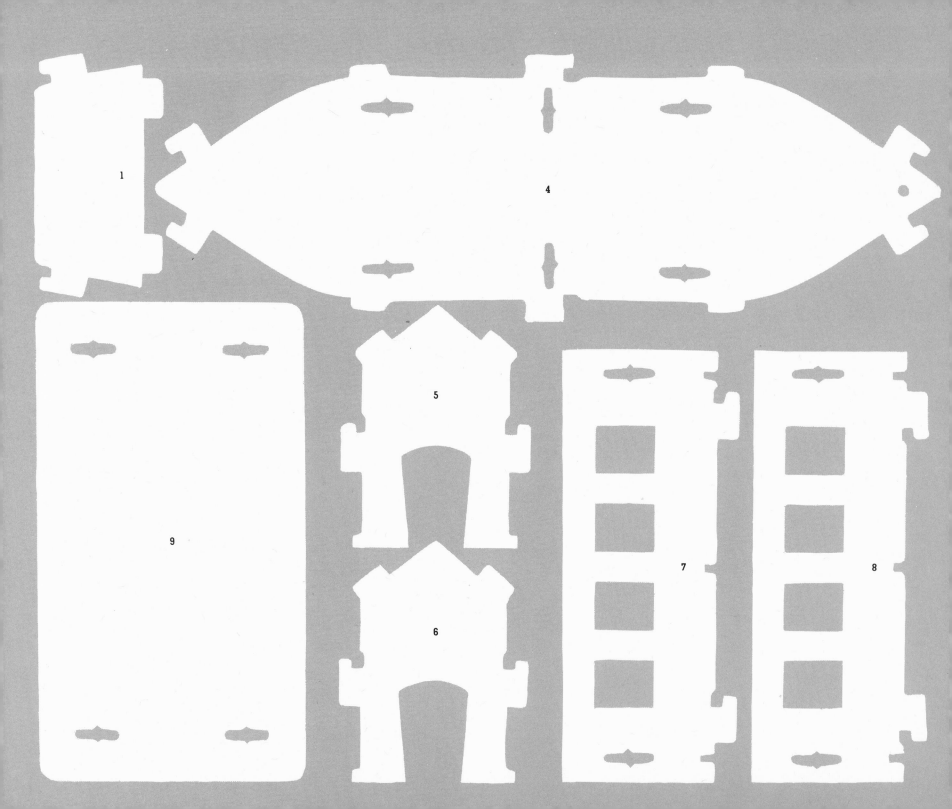

Cut out worksheet from this side.

Cut out worksheet from this side.

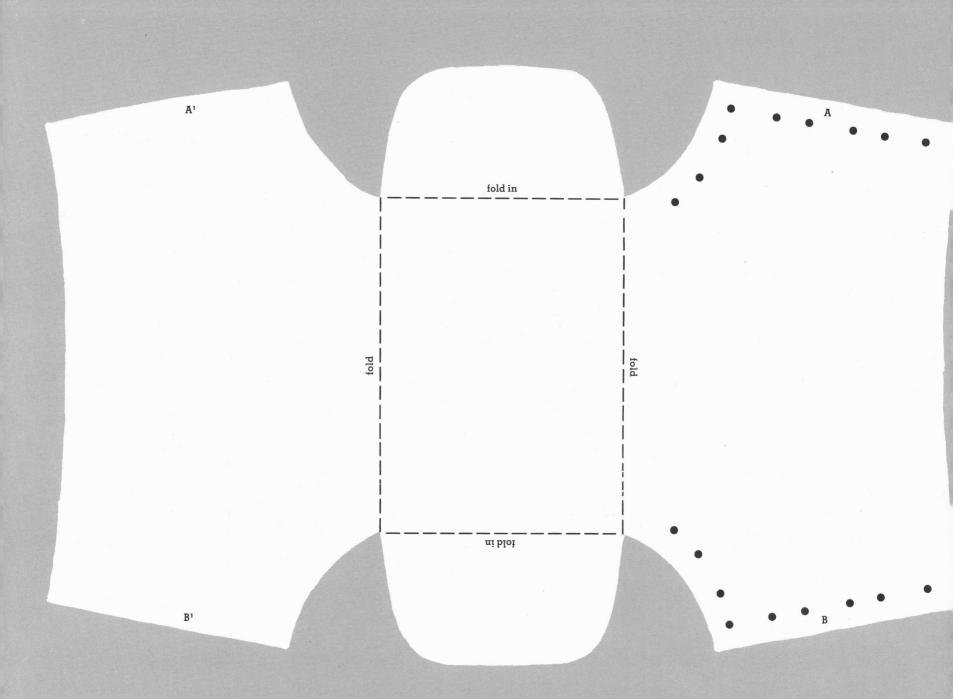

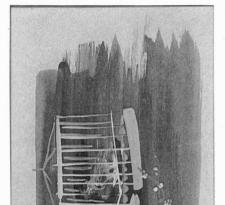

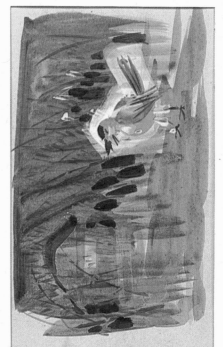

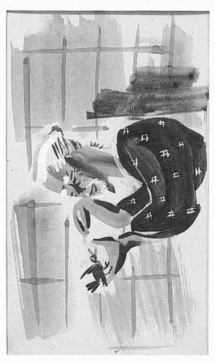

Cut out worksheet from this side.

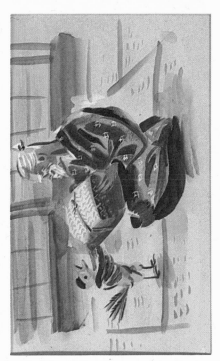

16

14

12

10

15

13

11

9